ജ *The Nine Tower of Ku* ൽ

<u>Fiction Series</u>

The Alex Evercrest Series
The River Front
The Girl on The Grill
Missing
Maggot
Racist
Votive Candles
Windy City
Country Road
Pool of Blood
Sins of the Daughter
Body Parts
The Skull Collector
The Vanishing
The Shadow Fighter
Moonshine
Grief's Trajectory
The Magic Touch
Northern Lights
Alex Evercrest Heroine
Alex Evercrest Collection Two
New Direction
A Family Affair
Disruption
The St. Lebuinnus Church Murder

A Brian O'Neil Novel
Hawaiian Phoenix
Moon Curser
Death Broker

The Problem Solver Series
Solutions
Drug Lords
Border Crosser
The Problem Solver Collection

The Taelo Series
The Early Years
The Golden Feather
Journey of Discovery
Dangerous Passage
Condor Clan Slingers
Circumvention
The Journey of Sages
Collection
Future Leaders Journey

A Taelo Story
White Swan and Quiet Pheasant
The Child's Name
Floating Cloud
Quiet Rabbit
Busy Bee
Little Otter & Talking Wren
Broken Spear
Burley Bear & Meadow Flower
Taelo Story Collection

Science Fiction

The Savitar Series
Journey's End
Savitar
Confluence
Savitar Series Collection

The Door Series
The Door
Aliens We
The Endless Hole
The Swarm
Esoteric Journey
The Gentle Eye
The Door Series Collection

Bram Nielson Series
The Fold
The Message
Fold Wormhole
Negative Fold
Ripples in Time
Bram Nielson Collection

Single Science Fiction Books:
Current Past and Future
The Event
The Door
Viajante 7

https://www.remwriter95.net/

❦ *The Nine Tower of Ku* ❧
By: *Ron Mueller*

Around the World Publishing LLC
Cincinnati, Ohio

ISBN 13: 978-1-68223-966-7

Distributed by Ingram
Cover Picture by: Pi03@ShutterStock
Cover Design by: Ron Mueller

1 The Nine Towers

The pine forest seemed to surround the valley's splendorous red, yellow, and lavender wildflowers and encapsulate the nine towered castle like, tan brick mansion that was at the center. The mansion sat on a thousand-acre plot. The driveway to the house ran for close to a mile from a small local highway. The isolation of the place was why Liam had purchased the property. It was exactly what he needed to do the style of recruiting that he had in mind. He knew that this place would allow him to operate freely and effectively.

He had been given a free hand at how he carried out his assignment and did not have to report his actions to Laticia, his sympathetic, softhearted boss. Soft hearted except when it came to following the rules and the adherence to lawful protocol. She was too by the book for him so he kept her in the dark as much as he could.

Liam did not have any of that sensitivity. He was a patriot did what he needed to do to get things done. He did what he thought was good for the Country.

He sat on the stone precipice and took in the nine towers where he had chained eighteen drug distributors. It had taken him close to a year to carry out the task of getting the top distributors from nine major cities, so some of his guests had been chained in the house for a year. He wished he could have moved faster but he had kept them well fed and encouraged them to exercise.

His goal was to either enroll them in the elimination of key international agents or to eliminate them and find the dealers from their regions that would. The choice was to work for him or die. He had abducted his victims first on the west coast, then the east coast and finally down the middle of the country. He had seventeen young males of various heritage, color, social standing, and he had one very good looking but very obstinate young lady that he was going to enjoy whether she agreed to his demands or not. He smiled as he thought of her as the icing on the cake.

He had an additional top drug dealer from each coast and from St. Louis chained in the downstairs part of the house. They enjoyed the comfort of the main downstairs bedrooms that were located around the base of eight of the towers.

This day, he had packed a picnic lunch and had hiked to where he was sitting so that he could contemplate the action that he would be taking over the next few days. The seclusion of the house had given him the luxury of not having to hurry but now it was time to take action in a methodical and swift manner.

He knew that he would enjoy the action and did not care how his recruits chose their fate. They were probably not aware of the price of saying no but that was what made it so exhilarating for him. He knew and that knowledge seemed to glow in his mind and excite his entire body.

One choice gave him a recruit that he had bent to serve him. That choice was less appealing to him than a rebellious no, but it was the choice he needed to carry out his mission.

The other choice gave him the same enjoyable taste equivalent to a box of top-quality Danish chocolates melting in his mouth, when he pulled the trigger of his forty-five and blew their faces off as the bullet put into the back of their skull exited in the middle of their face taking the soft jelly of their brains with it. It so excited him that he often had to suppress ejaculation.

Even sex was less exciting than pulling the trigger and enjoying the pattern made on the floor or the far wall. He always stood for a few minutes to take in the splendor of the red and white splatter.

The field of wildflowers surrounding the mansion seemed to augment the colors that were floating in his mind as he contemplated the coming few days and played various scenes in his head.

He knew that he would have a fair number of defiant noes and that often the second person having seen the result of a no would readily say yes.

Each day he would take the yeses and put them on flights back to their home towns with the first set of instructions that they were to carry out. He figured it would take him three days to empty the nine towers.

He contemplated all yesses from the top distribution leaders. They most likely would hear the gunshots that followed the noes, and they were in their positions because they knew how to negotiate, were more interested in living and to have a chance to money, they would make than in being defiant.

Once his recruiting was done it would take him a day to clean the place and get it ready for the next cycle of recruits. The recruitment would end when he had a sufficient number of distributors following his orders. Once they were all in place, he would focus their distribution to get the drugs flowing to the foreign agents he would target. The drugs would be both legitimate and illegitimate. He had doctors on his payroll that would provide him the legitimate drugs and he would have his recruits deliver those drugs but with the desired modification that would make them deadly.

He planned to carry out the elimination of the foreign agents in a swift and deadly manner.

He finished his lunch and went back to the house.

He entered via the back door that led into a grand kitchen that featured a hooded six burner gas stove at the center. A massive refrigerator with a black exterior that matched the black marble that embraced the gas stove stood directly behind it.

Stainless-Steel clad pots and pans of every design hung on the left side of the stove and a large set of nonstick utensils hung along the other side.

A set of twelve premier knives rested in their oak wood holder to the right of the stove. It was definitely a kitchen that had been designed for a chef.

He walked around the island to the refrigerator and helped himself to a beer. He gave a laugh as he thought about the fact that he had a huge supply of hot dogs and eggs but not much else. He fed boiled eggs and hot dogs to his captives. He also threw in an orange and apple per day for each of them. They did not go hungry, but they did not get meals prepared by a chef.

He grilled steaks, baked potatoes, and made salads for himself and his three most important recruits. He intended to gain their support both through coercion and also by feeding them well. He wanted them to understand that he was not trying to muscle them into submission. They would have the same choice to make as those chained in the rooms above them, but he did not expect to shoot any of them. He expected them to be smart enough not to say no.

He put the water on for the hot dogs, took out the buns and condiments that were designated to the eighteen upstairs guests and added an apple for each.

The upstairs always got served first. That way he could focus on doing a good job with the four downstairs meals.

For his three downstairs guests and himself, he had the steaks marinating. He would dry fry them and then melt blue cheese over them. He had mashed potatoes to go with them as well as a large helping of asparagus spears. He would also provide each of them with a glass of beer.

He ate by himself. He did not want to have any social connection with any of them.

The next morning, he distributed the boiled eggs and an orange to the upstairs guests.

He prepared two over easy eggs and a large sausage patty for the downstairs breakfast.

This was the day that he would ask the crucial question to each of those that he held captive. He smiled as he thought about the fact that he was going to go by a FIFO order for all the people he had been holding in his human inventory.

He went upstairs and removed the breakfast dishes from each of the tower rooms. Then he returned to the first room where he was holding Orson Ambrose and Sebastian Cassidy who were his Seattle captives. He addressed them by their full names and told them it was time for them to choose to serve him or not. He had them kneel and stood behind them.

He pulled out his forty-five and asked Orson whether he was willing to do as he would be instructed to do.

Orson told him he was a bastard and should go to hell.

Liam smiled and pulled the trigger and watched the mix of blood, brains, and hair spray across the room. He stood for a long time enjoying the sight. He knew what the answer he would get from Sebastian and wanted to enjoy the answer he had received from Orson.

He stepped behind Sebastian and asked the same question.

Sebastian shook his head up and down indicating that he would do as told.

Liam pushed a mop and bucket in front of him and told him to clean up the mess his partner had made. He then pointed to a body bag that he carried into the room and told him to put his buddy into it and to clean the room. He let him know that he would be released and get to go home that afternoon.

His next two captives were the two from L.A., Elisa Amos, and Mateo Garcia. He went through the same routine. He was surprised that Elisa and Mateo both agreed to follow his orders. He had expected Elisa to say no to his request and had been prepared to take her to the bedroom before shooting her. Instead, he felt somewhat relieved that she had said yes. He had come to like her. She had a survivor attitude. He figured she would do well when she got back to L.A.

He informed the two of them that they would be returning to LA that afternoon.

His San Diego two, Thiago Bandello and Osvaldo Comonte ended up being a repeat of the first two. He shot Thiago and after enjoying the moment, gave Osvaldo the job of cleaning up and putting his buddy in a body bag.

He went to the next set of rooms that held the six that he had abducted along the east coast. Riggs Melville made the mistake of saying no. His buddy, Rowan, was eager to say yes.

The two from New York were both agreeable to doing as they were told.

It turned out that the Miami two followed the no-yes pattern and Dante Cruz ended up in the body bag.

He then went from the two in New Orleans, the two in St. Louis and the two in Chicago and got all yeses. He wondered if the shots from his forty-five had been heard by all those saying yes. He decided in the future to use a silencer so that he could get an honest answer to his question.

He then went downstairs and had the three leaders kneel in front of him. He asked the L.A. leader whether he would work with him to take out some bad international spies. He got the agreement that he had expected.

He let him know that he would be driven to the airport with four young drug runners. Two of whom were from L.A., one from Seattle and one from San Diego. He suggested that they all chat and agree to work together. They would all have first class tickets to L.A.

He did the same with the Miami leader and let him know that he would be flying out with four of the young drug runners.

He asked Mylo for his answer and then let him know that he would be leaving the grounds with six young distributors who seemed eager to be back in the field.

Unknown to Liam, a trespasser hunting rabbits and squirrels had been sitting almost in the same spot where he had lunch the day before. This hunter had heard the shots and had called in the shootings. The hunter was asked if he was sure about the shooting and that he should come to the station to put in a formal report. The hunter thought about it and decided that he might get sued for trespassing and decided to go back to his car and go home.

2 The Occupants

Orson could not remember a time in his life that he was not mad. His father had beaten him regularly for the smallest of excuses. His mother was a junky who was seldom coherent. He was often left on his own to feed himself whatever he could prepare. He ate lots of canned soups, peanut butter and jelly and salami sandwiches. He ran away from home at the age of twelve and never looked back.

He found home at a soup kitchen that let him work for some food and sleep in one of their cots that was available for the homeless. Then the soup kitchen closed, he was out on the street making his way as best he could. Dumpster diving was his main source of food.

He watched the drug pushers distributing and periodically getting into gun fights amongst themselves. Then one day the gunfight was all around him and one of the pushers died in his arms. Before dying he learned where his supplier could be found, he was also handed a roll of money to give to that supplier. It was more money than he had ever had.

It lasted him almost six months.

Then he went looking for the drug supplier. It wasn't hard to find him, but it was hard to convince him that he could be a good distributor and trusted to bring the cash back to him. He was given a high school as his distribution territory and was soon bringing in more money than had ever been produced there. He was rewarded by being assigned the local university where he had the same success. His final step up was to the central downtown area where he was just getting started when he was snatched off the street and put in the back of a panel truck into a cage.

His captor was a large dark-haired, bearded guy with piercing black eyes who simply said that he was going to be given the opportunity of a lifetime.

The real outcome was that he spent almost a year chained in a room with another Seatle drug distributor.

Sebastian had first met Orson in the Seattle city center where they were both distributing their drugs. They had territories adjacent to each other and agreed to cooperate and help each other. It turned out they had similar family experiences, so they related well to each other. To have ended up in the same cage in the back of a panel truck had been a surprise to both of them.

Orson was the angriest about having been kidnapped. Sebastian was upset but figured it did no good to get angry he wanted to get even. He wondered why and wondered what the reason might be for the kidnapping.

It had been almost a year and the only thing that he had gleaned during that time was that their kidnapper wanted he and Orson to become subservient to him. He knew that there were at least four more captives. Two he had learned were from the L.A. area and two were from San Diego. Elisa was the only female in the group, and she was a person that he would never want to have mad at him. And she was really mad at her abductor.

Elisa was not mad she was furious and was determined to take revenge on the person who had thrown her into a cage like an animal and then had kept her chained for close to a year. It was enough time that she had figured out how she would eventually repay her abductor. His size and capability would not prevent her from getting even. If he ever let her loose, she would wait until the moment he let his guard down. Then she would take him down and she would put him through much worse treatment that he was putting her through. She was no stranger to killing. She had buried both of her parents to repay them for their years of abuse. She had almost a year to examine various scenarios for her pay back and she kept adding tortures that she would inflict on him. If she managed to get him in her clutches, he would end his life blind, tongueless, earless and have no gentiles and he would be screaming as he died. Her pastime was visualizing each of the barbarous things she would do.

Mateo knew Elisa well and he knew not to get her mad. He had many a beer with her. He had been present when she was fondled by a drunk as they sat at the bar.

She had gone into action and had hit the guy in the throat and then when he fell to the floor, she had kicked him in the side of his head and stomped on his face. The EMT's had put him on a board and taken him to a local hospital where he remained for more than a month.

Elisa had ignored the entire process and had returned to nursing her beer as if nothing had happened.

He was surprised to find the two of them in the same cage in the back of a truck. Later and for almost a year, they had shared the same common area where they were chained by their ankles to two rings in the floor. He had listened to her describe all the things she planned to do to their capture. She had also warned him to agree to whatever conditions that they were given for their release. She said that saying no might be what got them killed.

Thiago had been walking along the broad walk enjoying the setting sun before going to distribute his wares when he felt a gun on his back and was told to walk into the parking lot where he was put into a cage in the back of a panel truck. He was surprised to see four other people in two other cages before the back doors were closed and everything went pitch black. He asked if he should start yelling. He heard a feminine voice advise him to keep quiet. He felt the truck moving and short time later it stopped. Not long after the back door opened, and a second person was put into the cage with him.

Osvaldo had been approached, shown a gun by the person standing in front of him and told that he should do as he was told or get shot. He figured he was being robbed and offered to give up the money he had. He had been told to keep it but to do as he was told. He had walked as directed to the back of a panel truck and had gotten in. He was put into a cage with a person who looked to be Mexican or from some Latin American area. He got in and said hi.

The doors were closed, and all was black and then the truck drove off. Several hours later the truck stopped, and the back doors were opened. Their abductor entered and introduced himself as a member of the CIA and let them know that they were being recruited and their cooperation would be the ticket for their release.

He then escorted them into the rest area bathroom and said that the next stop would be several hours away. He let them know that if they gave him any trouble, they would be left at the rest stop as a body for the police to find later. The ride lasted for two days and then they were taken into a house where they were separated two to a room and chained to rings that were in a central area between the two bedrooms. The central area was about ten by ten and had a table and two chairs.

A day after they had been chained, their capture came in with a cooler and said that it was a week's worth of food.

Osvaldo tried to figure out if he could get the chain off his ankle but realized that the clasp was held in place with a rod that had no key.

Riggs had just finished a bowl of fake lobster tail and spaghetti when a dark-haired guy sat down next to him and suggested that he accompany him out to the parking lot. He figured he was being robbed and wondered if he should try for his gun. But that idea was short lived, and he felt a gun pressed to his back and his thirty-eight lifted from the back of his pants. He was led to the back of a panel truck and told to get in. He took in the two other cages and figured that he was part of some drug distributor pick up scheme.

Not long after, the door opened again and a second person who he recognized as another distributor that he did not know personally but who had had seen on the street. He was put into the cage with him. He learned his name was Rowan.

Then there was a several-hour drive which had him wondering where they were going. A short time after the truck came to a stop, he found out from the person to be put into the next cage, Ezekiel, that they were in New York City. An eastern looking fellow was the next person put into the van. He introduced himself as Boaz and asked if anyone knew what was going on.

The drive that followed took them all the way down to Miami. It was a logistical nightmare of periodic stops at rest areas and eating take out from fast food restaurants. In Miami, the third cage was filled with a Dante Cruz and a Kenji Mochizuki. On the long drive that followed, the two of them shared the fact that they made most of their money during the spring break. They distributed so many drugs of every variety that the rest of the year seemed like vacation.

None of them had any clue where they were going but they all figured it had to be north. They talked and realized they were all drug distributors. All they had been told was that if they cooperated, they would live to do their country a big favor. The implied threat of saying no was very plain.

Dante and Kenji were the last to be taken from the panel truck and led into the house. Dante counted nine circular towers as he looked up at the house. He wondered who would build such a monstrosity. As he was being chained to the ring in the floor, he realized that he and Kenji would be sharing one of the towers. He wondered where in the country they were located.

The next day their kidnapper brought in a cooler and they were instructed to make the food last for the next week.

He listened to Kenji comment that his room had a bathroom and a shower. He made the point that it was a better place than the dive he had been living in, in Miami. He had to admit that he too had been living in a dive.

Ambrose was doing a booming business even though there was no parade currently underway in New Orleans. A large number of tourists were doing a crawl from bar to bar, and he was able to intercept them and almost do a continuous sell of his various drugs. He figured he was having one of his better evenings. Then a tall guy in a devil's mask stopped him and told him to walk with him. He was about to tell him where to go until he felt the gun poke him in the side. He was guided to a white panel truck and then put into a cage.

Not long after the back of the truck opened, and another person was put into the cage with him. For the few moments that there was light, he recognized his new cell partner was of Cajun origin. In the dark, he introduced himself and learned that his new partner was Enzo Beaufoy. He asked who the guy in the devil's masked was.

Ambrose said he had no clue, but he had interrupted one of his better distribution nights.

Enzo agreed and said that he was loosing lots of sales.

The ride lasted for a long time and when he was given a bag with a burger and fries, he was able to learn from the ad on the bag that they had arrived in St. Louis.

He learned that the two put into the next cage were Zyair Smith and Lev Gataki. Zyair was black and a native of East St. Louis and Lev said he was from Russia.

It was another long ride with two meal breaks and bathroom stops at rest areas. Ambrose kept the conversation going as they rode along and said that he thought they were going north.

His direction was verified by the address on one of the ads on their fast-food meal bags. It was collaborated when the next two persons were put into the third cell.

Braylon Corbyn said he was from the Chicago area where he had grown up. Mykel Holmes said his family was from England, but he had grown up on the south side.

It was a long ride but shorter than the day before until the truck stopped and Ambrose and Enzo were escorted into a place that looked like some sort of medieval castle. They were led up long stairs up to a room where they had ankle chains put on and were told that they would be there for a few days before they would need to make a very important decision. Ambrose figured the important decision would have only one correct answer. He was worried about the answer Enzo, who seemed to be offended by being kidnapped, might give.

3 Main Room Guests

*L*iam was relieved to have gathered the street dealers and have them in their chains. He was now faced with the last step of his recruiting plan. It was going to happen in rapid fashion, and he hoped it would be as clean as the previous effort had been. He anticipated that it could be more dangerous. It was not going to be as simple as walking up to them and putting a gun to their ribs. His next recruits were at the top of their organizations and were usually surrounded by bodyguards. He planned to follow his west coast, east coast, and middle of the country abduction pattern. He had picked up two of the lesser distributors in Chicago, but he was choosing to pick his middle of the country leader in St. Louis. He had no desire to directly engage the Chicago mafia. He needed street presence in Chicago but did not need to get involved with one of the more powerful drug organizations.

He reviewed his L.A. abduction plan. He knew the name and had studied Jack Ahearn, the person that was currently one of the top drug dealers in the city.

He had one habit that was critical for the abduction and that was his every Thursday walk along the beach front boardwalk. He was dropped off at one end and had one guard stay there and he had another guard drive to a street that came to the beach at the other end of the walk and take up a position there.

Jack then would causally walk leisurely along the boardwalk with a cup of coffee in hand.

Liam parked the panel truck that he had rented at the very end of the parking lot near to where the second guard was waiting. There was about one hundred feet of beach that he would need to cross to get to the street where the second bodyguard parked his car.

He got out and opened the back of the van and walked out to the front and leaned casually against the front grill. The warmth from the radiator on his back gave him the feeling of being embraced. He looked down along the walk where he could see a rather old man sitting on a blanket in the shade of a palm tree. He could just make out a series of T shirt shops and a café. There were numerous people bicycling along to the end and then most would turn around and go back the way they had come. He hoped that when Jack got to the end and got ready to make the walk back that there would be no bicyclists.

He was not sure why the walk was such an attraction, but he was glad that it was because it provided the least risky way to snatch this L.A. distributor. The key would be to hit the guard in the neck with his dart gun just as Jack turned to go back.

As Jack approached, Liam walked to the end of the walk. He shot the dart and watched as the bodyguard that was sitting on a vine covered wall of a condo fell back into the vine covered ground and disappeared. He almost burst out laughing when he saw what had happened, but he moved quickly to intercept Jack and then guide him to the van.

He was pleased that it was impossible to see the guard at the other end. He hoped that there would be a long delay until the drugged guard managed to get out of the bushes. He figured if that was the time frame, he and Jack would be sitting in their first-class seats on a flight back to Cincinnati.

He explained the situation to Jack and suggested that he cooperate, and he let him know that within a few day he would be back in L.A. unharmed.

Once back in the house, he got everything settled with Jack who did object to being chained and said that what he was being asked to do would be very financially attractive.

Liam pointed out that he was chained but he should relax and enjoy his accommodation that was first class, and he should consider it a couple-day vacation. It would be a chance for him let all concerns about the business evaporate.

He was then off to Miami where he hoped he would have as quiet of a kidnapping. He was informed that the drug leader, Mylo left his yacht every afternoon and walked to a bay side flower shop where he bought flowers for his wife and then returned to the yacht. Then he and two bodyguards walked to where his limo was parked and drove home.

Liam parked his rental van across a green lawn in an outer parking lot located on the land side entrance to the shopping area. He then walked over to where he waited near the flower shop. He watched as Mylo approached unescorted. He stepped a little behind and to his left and suggested that the two of them walk past the flower shop and continue across the lawn to the black van. He was pleased that Mylo took it all in stride. He asked if Liam knew who he was kidnapping.

Liam assured him that there was no mistake and that if he cooperated, he would be back in a couple of days.

It was a direct flight to Cincinnati that took a couple of hours. By dinner time Mylo was seated and talking to Jack as they each cut into their steaming roasted prime rib with mashed potatoes and roasted vegetables and compared notes as to their abduction. Liam offered them a glass of a private reserve Cabernet Sauvignon that they both accepted.

He figured he would have enjoyed sitting down with them, but he had to feed the eighteen chained folks upstairs and then get ready for his flight the next day to St. Louis. Getting ready meant laying out enough food for everyone for the next few days. He was at the point that he was eager to get this part of his setup over with. It was too much work to feed this many people.

He flew to St. Louis and once there drove his tan van to the neighborhood where the top distributor lived. This was going to be a kidnapping that was to take place on the driveway leading up to Harper Bardin's residence. Harper had the habit of being dropped off at the end of his driveway and then walking the thousand or so feet up the hill to the front door of his house. Harper had a beautiful wife and two daughters. He had guards at the house but none of them were out on the grounds.

Liam had found the blind spot of the security camera system and had positioned himself in the bushes along the driveway. He watched as Harper was dropped off and the car drove off. He waited until Harper walked up to where he was parallel to him and then quietly asked him to step his way peacefully or die on the driveway.

Harper looked at him and asked if he was ready to die himself because he was making a big mistake.

Liam nodded and asked him to refrain from making threats and to step into the bushes with him. He disarmed Harper and then led the way to the point in the fence where he had created an opening wide enough for them to step through. He led the way to the van and put Harper in the front seat and closed the door. It had the child proof switch activated so Harper could not open the door while he went around and got into the driver's seat.

He explained that he would be back in less than two days and that he should relax and enjoy the ride. He let Harper know that he was going to be meeting his equals from St. Louis and Miami and would have a chance to make deals that would connect his network to distributors to both the east and west coast of the country.

The trip back to Cincinnati was uneventful and soon after Harper was talking to the other two distributors and comparing notes. The three of them seemed to get along well.

Liam let all three know that after a dinner of grilled picanha, with a side of rice covered with feijoada, fried plantains and mushrooms, followed by a dessert of cherry cobbler, he would share what he would be asking them to help him with. He assured them that their participation would enrich all of them and for the time they were working with him they were assured that no law enforcement agencies would bother them.

They asked who he worked for. He said that would remain an unknown to them, but they should be assured that he had the support of his hierarchy that any deal he made with, and they accepted, would put them off limits from local law enforcement. He then explained that he wanted to focus their distribution efforts to some key individuals that he wanted to either deport, arrest, or eliminate. The three of them would be asked to be of help in all three of those efforts. The eliminate action would be by making sure that if the person was using, he or she would receive a dose of drugs that was potent enough to kill them.

Harper chuckled and said that seemed to be easy enough since that often happened anyway with his current customers.

Mylo nodded and added that he would need to recruit the specific field individuals that would be the deliverers of the drugs.

Liam said that he had eighteen young recruits that he was holding upstairs. Each of the three of them had two of their own and then there were four more from their coast that each of them would be instructing. He painted the picture of how the three of them would have representation along the coast where they were located or along the Mississippi river from New Orleans to Chicago. He pointed out that they would be able to quietly increase their distribution regions.

He handed them their first-class tickets back to their cities. He said that he would give them the tickets for those going home with them, but he needed to go upstairs and verify who that was going to be.

It took him less than thirty minutes to return and hand each of the tickets for those going with them. He gave four to L.A. to Jack, he gave four tickets to Mylo to Miami and then he handed six tickets to St. Louis to Harper.

He smiled and said that he should have used a silencer so that he would have gotten honest answers from everyone.

The three of them nodded and commented that they were all glad that they had said yes.

Liam hand them their keys to their locks and then a hacksaw. He asked that they follow him upstairs to where their field workers were chained and that unlike their keyed ankle clasps the ones upstairs had been keyless pins that needed to be cut. He chuckled and said that it would be a chance for the three to be the humble servants to their workers. They should think of it as a biblical moment.

He had each group strip their beds and bring the linen down to the laundry area. He also had the four bodies carried and placed in a wagon that he had brought around with the tractor and parked by the back door in anticipation of having a few noes.

He had removed the cages from the panel truck and had put in bench seats that would hold all of them. He then drove them all to the airport.

Once he was back, he drove the tractor out into the woods where he had a backhoe to dig a deep grave into which he placed all the bodies.

He had one more series of recruiting to do before he was ready to focus on snagging the foreign operatives he was after.

4 The Request

The last case had ended only a week ago and Alex had focused on the firing range, flying her drone, and riding her bicycle on street patrol. The entire team was taking her lead and doing similar things. Bill and Trevor chose to drive around versus ride bikes, but Trey and Johnnie accompanied her wherever she went. They always met for lunch at a place that Johnnie got to choose.

It was one of their quieter weeks that they had enjoyed for as long as anyone of them could remember. Trevor was the one that commented that he was worried that it was the quiet before a storm. Soon after he had uttered that phrase, the Chief called them all into his office.

The Chief shared with them that he had received a call from the Ohio State Deputy Attorney General for Law Enforcement, Cynthia O'Reily, asking if she could get Alex to examine a very unique, unusual, and concerning situation just outside of Logan, Ohio.

He pointed out that the departments reputation for solving cases had caught the eye of state law enforcement leaders and that went a long way in ensuring that they would get the budgetary funds the department needed. He suggested that they take the police van and all five of them drive to Logan and meet with the Highway patrol officer in charge of a home in the middle of the forest being guarded and sealed off as a crime scene.

On the way out to the van Trevor commented that he should not have mentioned the calm before the storm. Bill chuckled and said they had no clue what they were being asked to look at and Trevor had no clue about any storm. He hoped that they would be able to clear things up just by looking. He then added that he doubted it. He figured they had weathered many a storm together and would do so again.

Alex said that they should all go prepared for the worst and that meant they would wear their protective Kevlar outfits when they got there.

The drive to the Logan area took about two hours. Johnnie kept updating them and then as they got close, he gave Trevor the detailed directions on how to get to the house where they were to meet the Highway patrol who was handling the investigation.

The drive up the small gravel lane, through a dense forest of maples, oaks and smaller cedars seemed to be leading them back in time.

Bill commented that the location was very secluded.

Trevor stopped the van when the house came into view. He counted the circular turrets and when he reached nine, he commented that nine was connected biblically to the ninth Psalm that predicts the coming of the Antichrist. He went on to say that the number nine was also said to be ruled by the Planet Mars and he made the point that the orange brick should have been red to give the home good luck, so he figured bad luck was at hand. He then added that in Japanese the word for nine was "ku" which is similar in meaning to "pain or suffering" and therefore associated with bad luck.

Bill asked him how he knew so much about the number nine.

Trevor smiled and said that he was born on September the ninth in nineteen fifty-nine and so he had been fascinated with the number nine all of his life.

Alex smiled and said she was glad that there were no nines in her birth date and suggested they get up to the house to check whether the nine towers had anything with them getting called in.

The Highway patrol leader introduced himself as Clay and said that he had never investigated a situation that seemed quite as weird as what he had found in each of the towers of the house as well as in the downstairs living area. He led the way in and turned right into an area he said they were calling "the downstairs ring and chain area" where there were three chains with locking leg irons. He pointed to the anchor points out and said that the chains were long enough to allow whoever was locked in them to reach the bedrooms and the bathrooms.

He then led the way upstairs and said that there were two leg iron chains in each of the nine towers, but they did not have locks but rather had leg irons that were put on with pins that were hammered into the leg irons. He pointed to each of the rooms and said that each room had clean bed sheets and bedding as if they were to be used in the near future.

Alex asked how the Highway Patrol had been called in.

He said that a hunter had called some shootings in but had waited a day to report what he claimed was gun fire coming from the house. This hunter had waited a day to come in and give his report because he was concerned about being sued for trespassing, but he was so sure that there had been gunfire in the house and knowing that he had convinced himself to take a chance and make the report.

Alex asked to see each of the rooms. She walked to the doorway of each and looked in. Then she returned to the first and laid down outside of the door and looked across the floor. She did this for each of the rooms and then returned to the first one and did it again.

Clay asked Trey what his partner was doing. Trey replied that she was looking for differences between the rooms because if there had been gunfire that had killed someone then there would have been a clean up to remove the blood. She was looking to see if there were differences between the rooms.

Clay commented that he and his troops had not found any blood anywhere.

Alex stood up and said that she wanted a forensics specialist called in to closely examine towers number one, three, four and six because they had been cleaned more than the other tower rooms. She expected there to be some indication of blood in them.

Clay asked one of his officers to arrange for a team to come in and check out the towers for blood.

She then asked Trevor and Bill to go out and find a wagon or other transport that could move bodies to some sort of burial ground.

She asked Johnnie to launch Gunjfor and see if he could locate where the burial of any bodies might have occurred.

Clay asked what made her think there would be buried bodies anywhere in the vicinity.

Alex smiled and said that she had no idea if there would be any bodies, but it was likely if the person who had made the report had heard gunfire that there would be at least some bodies. And she said that she was betting on four bodies that were buried somewhere. The chains indicated that whoever had been on them were not there willingly.

Not long after, Bill called her and let her know that he and Trevor had found a tractor hooked to a wagon that could have been used to transport bodies.

Clay nodded and said that his men had found the tractor in the barn, but it was clean and had not raised any flags.

Bill had been listening and commented that it seemed that the wagon had been hosed off before being put into the barn.

Alex asked Bill and Trevor to see if they could find any tractor tire marks leaving from the rear of the house and going somewhere.

Johnnie called in a few moments later and said that he thought he had found a grave that had been recently dug and then camouflaged. He gave them all directions from the house and suggested that shovels be brought out.

Clay again asked how a grave could be found so easily.

Trey commented that the entire team had learned to identify graves in the forest in a case where they went along the entire US-Canadian border identifying them and Johnnie was the best among them in using his drone in finding them. He suggested they take several shovels.

Trevor called in again and said that they had also found a baby backhoe that he thought they should drive out to make the digging easier. He asked if any of Clay's people knew how to use it.

Clay left and returned a few moments later with one of his men who said he knew how to operate the baby backhoe. He also had three additional men with shovels.

He commented that the situation was getting worse than he had thought.

They all rode the wagon out to where Johnnie was standing in the woods.

Once the leaves and brush were cleared off, it was clear that there was what appeared to be a filled in grave.

The backhoe dug slowly down to a full six feet. Then it snagged a thick black plastic bag. The driver of the backhoe backed away from the hole and got out and suggested that someone with a shove get into the hole to clear the dirt off the bag.

Alex asked everyone to stop. She said that she would like the body removed and transported to Cincinnati where she would have it examined by Dr. Rogers. She asked if he could make that happen.

Clay said that he had been told to do whatever she asked so he would arrange for the transport.

Alex asked that he also expedite the detailed examination of the towers she had identified but that everything in the house get a new detailed examination with the knowledge that at least one murder had been committed.

She said that the team was going back to Cincinnati and do some research on the property, and anyone listed as the owners.

Bill was doing the driving and Trevor was doing the talking about the fact that they had only found one grave.

Alex answered her phone and put it on speaker mode when she learned it was a call from Clay. He had called to let her know that four bodies had been lifted out of the single grave.

The bodies had been loaded into a hearse and were on the way to Cincinnati. He had instructed the persons transporting the bodies to deliver them to the main downtown police station. She thanked him for the heads-up and for how fast he was able to make that happen.

He chuckled and said that he did not want to spend the night at the crime scene site but wanted to get home to his family and enjoy dinner.

After hanging up Alex called Dr. Rogers to let him know to have his team be ready to receive the four bodies.

She then called the Chief and brought him up to speed on what the team had found and that he should declare it as a murder case called "The Nine Towers of Ku."

The Chief laughed and said that he was very interested how she had come up with that name.

Alex replied that Trevor was to blame and that he should talk to him about the number nine and all of its meanings.

She let him know that in the morning she and the team would get him up to speed on everything they had found out so he could communicate back to Cynthia O'Reily and the rest of the state's hierarchy.

5 Autopsy Trail

Alex walked her bike across the walkway to downtown that went over the various interstate highways below it. She was thinking about the case that she felt had a very creepy feeling to it. Who would chain up twenty-one people in a house for some reason and then shoot four of them.

She hoped that Dr. Rogers would provide some sort of clue that would help unravel the mystery that spread like a blank landscape across her mind. Once off the walkway she got on her bike and headed to meet up with Johnnie. The two of them met every morning outside of her old apartment build where he was still living and rode in to the station together. They each wore a headset that allowed them to chat on the way in. This morning, they discussed the weird aspects of the case. They were both in agreement that they needed to get some clue from Dr. Rogers because so far, they had found a murder crime scene but had no clue as to who the criminal might be.

Johnnie commented that he was going to dig into the property ownership and see what he could find out about who owned it.

Once they arrived at the station, Alex changed into her work outfit of a black pant suit and jacket. She then stopped and got a cup of black coffee and walked out into the bull pen. She and Johnnie, as usual, were the first to get there.

Johnnie fired up his computer and commented that Dr. Rogers must have come in early because he had sent him the DNA of the four suspects and let him know that he also had dental imprints and hoped that they could be used as positive verification if the DNA didn't immediately identified the individuals.

Alex suggested that Johnnie begin his search with the DNA information while she went down to see the doctor. When she arrived, Dr. Rogers greeted her and pointed to the bodies that were laying on the examination tables. Each of them had their head covered. He said that there was not much of the face left but a gaping hole, but the mouth and jaw were almost left undisturbed. He said that he had found two forty-five slugs loose in the body bags. He wondered where the third and fourth slugs had ended up.

Alex asked about the condition of the slugs and learned that they were slightly disfigured but from his examination it was clear that the gun that had fired the bullet was within inches of the back of the head.

Dr. Rogers said that this meant that the slug only made a small hole going in but literally blew out the entire forehead as it came out. The shooting had been execution style with a slight downward angle. He postulated that the person being shot was kneeling and the person pulling the trigger was standing behind

From those two suppositions he figured the person doing the shooting was six foot to six foot two inches tall.

Alex asked if he might also have the shooter's skin complexion, hair, and eye color.

"Yes, I will send that up in my next report," Dr. Rogers jokingly answered.

Alex asked if he was willing to go to the crime scene and do a detailed examination where the shootings had taken place.

Dr. Rogers said that he and his team would welcome doing so. It would help him answer a lot of questions that was running through his mind.

Alex suggested that they make a day trip to the site where the shootings had taken place and that they leave later in the morning. She then returned to the bull pen where everyone was sitting and getting started. She accepted half of a bear claw from Trey and after taking a bite and a sip of coffee said that they should all meet in the huddle room right after she brought the Chief up to date on the case.

The Chief waved her to the chair in front of his desk and asked for her update.

The update was short, precise as she explained why she had asked him to label the case, "The nine towers of Ku." She explained that it appeared that up to twenty-one people had been chained in those towers and four had been shot and killed while still being chained.

The Chief shook his head and said that his best two teams were constantly getting involved in cases that stretched his imagination. He added that the department had benefitted financially from their efforts and managing the budget had gotten easier, especially after she had stopped having her police cars shot up, blown up or burned to a crisp..

Alex laughed and remined him that she had not been the one to blow up, set her car on fire or turn it into Swiss cheese. She reminded him that she had been the victim.

He smiled and said that all he knew was that it had cost him being able to hire another investigative team so that he could keep wheels under her.

She let him know that she and the team were heading back to the scene of the crime, and she had convinced Dr. Rogers to take his team to the site and do a thorough examination.

The examinations of the four rooms where Alex thought the shootings had occurred led Dr. Rogers team to find the third and fourth bullets lodged in the wall. They had gone unnoticed because one had lodged at the very center of a black-eyed Susan flower in the wall paper and the other wall was covered with an arrangement of various colored spots.

The bullets had enough blood on them that Dr. Rogers felt certain he would be able to determine which of the four bodies had met their end in each of the towers. He then commented that the cleanup in tower number one had not been thorough, and his team had found blood on the wall.

They found that though the floor had been cleaned there was evidence of blood in all four towers that Alex had identified. He had his team also looking for any hairs, skin droppings or finger nail clippings that might provide DNA of the occupants of all the rooms. He commented that they would most likely be gathering evidence for the rest of the week.

Alex examined the contents of the refrigerator and noted that there seemed to be two different menus for the occupants, hot dogs, and steaks. Given the ratio of the food in the frig she speculated that those held up in the towers had survived on hot dogs and the three held in the main floor had dined on steaks and baked potatoes. This was an indication to her that the upstairs prisoners were of a lesser status than those held downstairs.

She glanced at the trash can and asked Trey to put on gloves and pick up the top cover to see what was inside. She pointed to a set of discarded gloves and said that Dr. Rogers would most likely be able to get finger prints from the inside surface.

She went into the living room and noted that the coffee table near the couches were glass topped. She glanced down through the glass and pointed to finger prints on the bottom surface of the glass. She put a crayon circle on the top side so that Dr. Rogers' team would easily find them.

She was becoming more confident that they would crack the case. She figured that the hunter had caused the investigation to begin before the perpetrator had been prepared, otherwise she was sure that the place would have been cleaned more thoroughly and that no clue would have been found.

She asked Johnnie to expand his search for signs of any absent drug dealing leaders.

She noted that the marks on the floors up stair indicated that those captives had been held longer than the three held downstairs where there were no wear marks on the rug or floor.

She then took a walk out to the barn where the tractor and baby backhoe were once again parked. She looked over both pieces of equipment and the wagon as well and commented that all three pieces looked rather new and not weather worn as farm equipment often did. She added finding out when and where they had been purchased to the list of things that needed to be followed up on.

She pointed at the fifty-gallon gasoline drum that that was mounted on a stand. She wondered if the gasoline had been purchased by the barrel. That would mean that some gas station nearby would have noted a fifty-gallon sale. Buying gas for the two units might be another avenue that could help identify the person or persons that lived in the house.

She went back into the house and asked Dr. Rogers to be especially thorough in processing everything in the fourth downstairs bedroom. She added that she thought the person in charge of the entire operation had used it.

She asked Johnnie to locate a local pizza shop where she could order enough food for everyone working the crime scene.

Clay, the Highway patrol leader had quietly followed Alex around and had been impressed with her thorough search for evidence. He was amazed at the wide net she was throwing to identify the perpetrator and the fact that she believed it was just one individual. He had expected that several people would have been involved but it was now clear to him that the search was narrowing down to one person.

When he heard her getting ready to order pizza for everyone he spoke up and said that he knew of a great pizza shop in Logan and suggested using them. He would send a couple of his men in to bring the pizza back.

Alex thanked him and suggested that they get one pizza for every two persons at the site and enough drinks to match.

She then asked if there were any gas stations where a person might fill a fifty-gallon drum and not get noticed.

Clay shook his head and said that the site was only about forty miles from Columbus where there were numerous places to buy fifty gallons and not be noticed but that buying that much at any gas station closer to their location would be noticed.

Alex asked about places to buy the farm equipment and was pointed to two places that were withing a few miles of where they were.

He added that the gas could have been part of the sales deal since these places made sure that the purchaser would be able to run the equipment immediately. They would also try to set up refill services to sweeten the sale.

The pizza arrived and Alex led the way to a large maple tree and spread out a blanked that she carried in the back of her car. During lunch she asked Bill and Trevor to check out the places that sold farm equipment. She asked Johnnie to continue his research into ownership of the property.

She was going to see if she could get finger prints that would allow them to close in on the person who had set up a very elaborate kidnapping scheme. She was beginning to suspect that the amount of money that such venture took could only be funded by a well-financed organization, and she thought it was too complex for any of the drug runners to set up. She was suspecting one of the US government organizations.

Trevor commented that once again they were well outside the scope of a normal crime and into the netherworld of secret government organizations. He made the point that killing individuals was a step to the dark side and highlighted a person that might have gone rogue. It would be a very talented person who when they closed in could become violent. What made it worse it seemed that he had the money to do whatever he desired to do.

Johnnie nodded and said that he would see if he could find such an individual and when he did, he would cut them off from the ability to easily get to the cash. He said that if he had the finger prints that were probably in the gloves, he would be able to identify him.

Alex said that she would get Dr. Rogers to process the gloves immediately so that they could get to the perpetrator as quickly as possible.

6 Derailed

*T*he police cars flashing lights at the end of the driveway caused Liam to drive slowly by. He did not know exactly what the cars were doing there but he was sure that in meant that his house had been discovered. He drove on and parked the van out of sight in the forest near where he had buried the four that he had shot just a week ago. He carefully walked to where the grave was located and was surprised to find that it had been dug up. He stood looking down into the grave trying to think through what he had to do next.

He had six abductees from Texas and now he had no place to put them. He looked down into the grave and thought about his next step. He decided that it was time for him to move on and find a totally new place from which to operate.

He realized that it was a setback, but he still had the three main drug distribution regions under his control and eighty percent of the foreign operatives he was after resided in those locations.

He decided that he had to get rid of the six that he had in the van and move on.

He told himself that he hated to do it, but he would have to get rid of six that he had just driven up from Texas and that it wasn't fair to them, but it was not his fault that he had no place to house them. He thought about the deep ravine not far from where the van was parked. He would take them two at a time, off them and push them down into the ravine. He figured that they would probably not be found for months or maybe never. He moved the van close to the ravine and then two at a time he marched them to the edge and then shot them from behind. It was over in less than five minutes.

He was disappointed that he had not had the time to enjoy disposing of them. He looked around and found several dead limbs that he threw down into the ravine in hopes that the bodies would not be visible unless one was actually in the ravine. Early on when he first purchased the property, he had tried entering and walking the ravine and found it almost impossible, so he figured that the bodies were there for a long duration.

He returned to the truck and thought about next steps. He had his weapons, his travel suitcase and access to his accounts. He could set up his headquarters wherever he desired. He would send in reports to his boss that things were going as planned and he would soon be apprehending the spies.

He decided to operate out of New Orleans since he liked the Cajun cuisine, and it was a partying city that catered to a great number of strangers. He would be able to operate there and never be noticed.

In Tennessee he stopped and got rid of the panel truck and bought a used tan sedan. He drove on and when he got to Mississippi, he traded cars again and chose a black Cadillac that he drove on to New Orleans. He knew a place near the river where he could rent a rather comfortable condo that was modest but comfortable and it would allow him to walk to the park along the river. He would be moving into his elimination of spies mode and would need the use of his computer more than anything else. He wanted a good view from his work desk, and he wanted to be near some good restaurants.

He looked around his third-floor room and sat down at the desk that was in the rounded corner of the room that overlooked the open area with a grey stone and brick circle where two walking streets crossed just below.

His two-bedroom condo was all on the same floor and went from the corner room, two rooms wide, to the other end of the condo. The entire condo was twenty-five hundred square feet in size. It had a central open area where the kitchen and eating area took up most of the space. The eating area faced the exterior and had a small terrace where one could sit and enjoy the outdoors.

He was glad that he had the funds to enjoy what many would have considered a luxury. He considered it essential to his wellbeing.

He went up on the roof and found a way to leave that took him over two roof tops and to a fire escape that led down into a secluded alleyway. This gave him confidence that he would not get trapped in his condo if he were to be confronted.

Because he had lost his computer at the house of nine turrets, he had to reestablish all of his computer network connections. Setting all of his connections back up was challenging and time consuming. He hoped that his computer that he had left behind would not be found but he was not too worried if it was found because it had so many layers of encryption that it would be impossible for anyone to get anything useful from it.

At the same time, he was getting re-established, Alex and the team were back at the crime scene. They had done their initial search of the nine turrets and were discussing what they might be missing.

Trey commented that they had not found any indication of what the purpose of having people chained and held captive meant or why it was done. He commented that the place was too clean and that even though their involvement seemed to have disrupted what was going on they had not found any damming evidence other than the grave with four bodies. He wondered why the house seemed so sterile.

Bill said that he agreed. It seemed that a phantom had been running the place.

Trevor asked if he meant spook as in some secret government operative.

Alex said that could be one explanation and they should begin looking for convenient places to hide the damming evidence. She asked Trevor and Bill to check all vents in the bedroom used by whoever had run the place and then do it in every downstairs vent. She and Trey would hunt for a hiding place in the kitchen and downstairs dining room.

Not long after, Trey discovered a very thin lap top computer hidden on the top shelf of the pantry. It had bottles of spices stacked on top of it and was not visible. He only discovered it because he was standing on a footstool and methodically taking all the spices off the shelf.

He handed that computer down to Alex who had been going through the under the counter shelves searching through pots, pans, and a large number of lids.

She said that she would ask Johnnie to see if he could get into it and see what he could find.

Johnnie had been out on the grounds flying Gunjfor and looking around the property from the air. He had wandered out to the edge of the property and had discovered a rather deep crevasse and began to explore it.

He walked over to the edge of the crevasse but stepped back and sat down on a fallen log and took Gunjfor carefully down toward some limbs that seemed out of place relative to the rest of the crevasse that he could see.

Then he saw an arm and as he took Gunjfor closer he could make out a body. He was able to see another pair of shoes and knew that he had found at least two bodies. He brought Gunjfor back up and put her away. He called to let Alex know that he had found more bodies and that it was going to take some special effort to retrieve them.

He let her know that he was walking back to the house because he need to replace Gunjfor's batteries.

Alex walked up to where Dr. Rogers and his team were still processing the tower rooms and let him know that Johnnie had found more bodies.

She then let Clay know that there were bodies down in a ravine and that between he and Dr. Rogers they needed to decide how to proceed to get them out of the ravine.

The entire team was waiting when Johnnie returned. He put up his hands and said that he needed to replace Gunjfor's battery and put the one she had used to charge back up so she could be used to provide a closer view of the bodies he had found.

He then opened his computer and played back what he had seen in the ravine.

Clay commented that it would take a helicopter to lift the bodies out of the ravine.

Dr. Rogers added that he wanted his team to go down into the ravine to examine the bodies before anything was disturbed. He asked if Johnnie could get some shots of the entrance to the ravine so he could decide how his team would get to the bodies.

Johnnie led them to the ravine where he set up his computer on the fallen tree. He then launched Gunjfor and took her down to the entrance of the ravine and flew her up toward where the bodies were located.

Dr. Rogers shook his head and said it looked impossible to hike up to the place where the bodies were located and that it looked like his team would need to be lowered down from the helicopter.

Clay said that the chopper was on its way from Columbus and would be arriving in the next half hour.

Dr. Rogers led his team back to the house where they got into some protective gear and got ready to go down into the ravine. He made sure they had their cameras and field equipment so they could examine the bodies before moving them. He point out that it was a risky assignment and if any of them had any issues they should say something.

Meanwhile Alex let Johnnie know about the computer that Trey had found and that after the recovery of the bodies, she wanted him to see what he could learn by getting into the computer.

Johnnie smiled and said that he was moving up from cookies to riverside steak meals as a reward for the magic she wanted him to deliver.

Alex put on a sad face and asked if he was getting tired of her baking him cookies.

Johnnie shook his head and said that his request was in addition to the cookies. He said that he was just hungry because of all the hiking he had done so far, and he really wanted something different than more pizza.

Trevor spoke up and said that he and Bill were done searching for hiding places in the house and that they could make a lunch run and get whatever everyone wanted.

Alex suggested that they specifically get what each of them wanted. She added that she was going for a salad with a salmon topping.

Once everyone had made their selection Trevor and Bill asked Clay for the name of a restaurant that would have the menu that would match the choices made. They then called in the order and said that they would return with everyone's lunch.

The helicopter arrived as Bill drove out. He commented that he was glad to be making the lunch run and hoped that the bodies were out of the ravine by the time they got back.

Alex, Trey, Johnnie, and Dr. Rogers stood by the edge of the ravine as two members of Dr. Rogers team was lowered down to the bodies. Once down they let everyone know that there were more than two bodies and from what they could tell the ones they could see had been executed in the same manner as the ones they had dug up.

They said that it looked as if they had been shot and then dumped into the ravine because the areas where the bone were protruding did not have much blood from the broken bone areas. They suggested having the bodies lifted and taken to an examination area where a closer examination could be made.

During the preparation to lift the first body, the two down in the ravine were able to verify that there were six bodies to be lifted out.

Dr. Rogers asked Clay if one of his people could drive the morgues van as close to the ravine as possible and to let the helicopter pilot know where to take the bodies that were lifted out of the ravine. It took about forty-five minutes to lift the bodies out and get the Dr. Rogers two people out of the ravine.

Dr. Rogers had done a preliminary examination of the bodies as each got lifted from the ravine. When the last arrived, he reported that they had all been killed in the same manner as the four he had examined previously. They were all male in their early to mid-twenties and they had most likely been killed in the last two days. He added that he needed to get them back to his lab so he could do a more detailed analysis.

Bill and Travis drove in with lunch as Dr. Rogers and his team were getting ready to transport the bodies back to Cincinnati.

Since most of his team had ordered steak or something other than a sandwich, Dr. Rogers decided they should eat and then drive back to Cincinnati.

Johnnie meanwhile had tried getting into the computer that Trey had found and commented that it was password protected, it was going to be a challenge to get into it so he might need to do it once they got back to the office.

Alex shook her head and said that it seemed that the discovery of the bodies and the computer was redirecting the team's focus.

She talked with Clay and asked him to keep the area secured and monitored until she released it. She doubted that the killer would return but figured the area needed to be kept as a crime scene until it was fully processed.

She called the Chief and caught him up on what had happened and let him know that everyone from Cincinnati was on their way back. She commented that whomever they were after was a serious danger and a killer that seemed to kill without concern to doing so.

7 Tracking

Once back in the office, Alex watched over Johnnie's shoulder as he worked at getting into the computer. First, he had to get past the password needed to turn it on. He tried the normal approach to turning on the computer for a few moments but then he plugged in a thumb drive prior to restarting the computer so that the Password Re-format routine that he had coded would invade the memory of the computer as it powered up and let him put in the password that he had chosen.

Alex asked him what password he had chosen.

He laughed and said that it was her first name because she managed to open up all doors or obstacles that got in her way.

Trey had been sitting quietly but started laughing when he heard the exchange.

Once Johnnie had the computer open, he ran into the next barrier in that all the files were encrypted and required administrative permission to get in.

He opened up another one of his hacking routines that searched for the administrators name and when he had it, he then opened all files. It took him the rest of the day to work his way to the point that he was able to begin to browse through the information that was stored on the computer.

He decided to transfer the entire content of the laptop to one of the departments computers and make a copy for himself as well. He then turned off the laptop and closed it.

Bill came into the huddle room and said that he was not sure what was going on but three people acting like they were in control had been escorted into the Chief's office. He added that the lady leading the group appeared to be upset and on a mission. Since they were the only ones handling an unusual situation, he thought he would sound the alarm.

A few moments later, the Chief's support poked her head into the huddle room and said that the Chief wanted everyone in his office.

Alex said she would be right in. She turned to Johnnie and asked if he had what they wanted off the laptop. He said that he had a duplicate of everything including the operating system and every bit and byte that was on the computer. She nodded and said that was good and asked him to bring the lap top with him.

She called down to Dr. Rogers and asked him to copy all of his information about the bodies he had processed and put the information on a thumb drive for her. He was not to say anything about the thumb drive when they all came to the morgue.

He asked what was up.

She let him know that she thought the CIA, or some similar entity had just arrived and might be in the mood to shut down what the department was working on.

She led the team to the Chief's office and the five of them entered.

The Chief introduced Laticia, Thermon and Jason as CIA agents that had come because the beacon from one of their laptops had triggered a signal that they had traced to the department. He asked Alex if she knew anything about that.

Alex said that the computer had been found at the site where nine bodies had been found. She added that so far, they had not had time to analyze the contents of the computer. She added that it was password protected.

Alex then asked why a CIA computer would be found at such a site.

Laticia replied that she was not able to provide a reason, but she wanted to get the computer back and wanted to know more about who the dead might be and how they had died.

Alex knew that she was about to lose both the computer and shortly be told that the dead bodies would be picked up by CIA representatives. She was anticipating being told to stop her investigation.

Laticia said that the deceased were most likely foreign spies that had been caught and resisted arrest and put up a fight of some sort.

Alex resisted sharing the facts that would refute such a situation.

When Laticia asked where the bodies were located, Alex replied that they were in the morgue getting processed.

Laticia looked at the Chief and said that all analysis of the bodies should come to a halt. She then said that she wanted to get a firsthand look at the bodies and then she would have them transferred to a morgue in the Capital for a more thorough analysis.

The Chief looked at Alex and saw the face he knew all too well. He knew that Alex had all she needed from the bodies and that she was not buying any of Laticia's condescending words. He wanted to laugh because he knew that whatever Alex was willing to give up was of no more use and that she had what was needed to solve her case. He led the way to the morgue.

When he entered the morgue, Dr. Rogers smiled and asked what all the people were doing coming into his lab.

Laticia introduced herself and said that she needed him to stop all work he was doing on the bodies, and she wanted all of his lab records that had to do with the bodies.

Dr. Rogers walked by Alex bumped into her and dropped the thumb-drive he had into her pocket and then walked over to his desk. He pointed to a box with ten files that had the information on the bodies and said that was all he had on the bodies. He added that he was just about to put it all into the departments computer but had been too busy to do so.

Laticia pointed to the box and asked Thermon to take it with him when they left.

She asked if she could see the bodies.

Dr. Rogers opened up four of the slide out morgue body holders and pulled the bodies out half way. He then lifted the cover over the first body to show the faceless individual.

Laticia seemed to take a step back and she collided with Johnnie who commented that the gun battle with the bad guys had not been fair.

It was clear she had not expected to see what she was looking at. She hesitated for a moment and asked what the cause of death had been.

Dr. Rogers shook his head and said that it was a forty-five bullet to the back of the head administered at a range of about two inches. Most likely when the individual was kneeling in front of the shooter.

It was clear that Laticia was surprised and that the story she had spouted about a gun battle did not fit the situation.

Johnnie, who had remained standing close to her, commented that it clearly had not been a fair fight. He quietly added that maybe it instead was an execution.

She asked about the other six deceased.

Dr. Rogers said that all of them had met the same fate in the same manner.

Laticia said that she would have the bodies transferred that afternoon and said that she had to get to the local office and make the arrangements. She looked at Thermon and Jason and said that it was time they got back to the office. She asked the Chief to guide them back to the entrance.

He nodded and looked at Alex and the rest of the group then asked them to meet him in his office.

She waited a moment until the Chief had left and then thanked Dr. Rogers for having been so efficient at his examination. She handed the thumb drive to Johnnie and told him to move the information to some system outside of the department and then erase the thumb drive. She also asked him to move the image of the CIA computer to an off-station computer as well.

Then she asked if he had gotten what he wanted by standing so close to Laticia.

Johnnie said that he would have all the information moved out of the department by the time they got to the Chief's office he just needed to borrow Dr. Rogers' computer for a few moments.

He sat down and connected to one of the many cloud accounts he had and transferred everything he had to an account he titled Nine Towers. He let Dr. Rogers know that when the computer beeped everything would be done and the thumb drive would be empty, and he could use it for another purpose.

He then looked at Alex and said that the team currently had no information about the lap top or the dead bodies in any official department computers.

Alex led the way back to the Chief's office.

The Chief asked what had taken them so long to reach the office.

Alex smiled and said that they were chatting with Dr. Rogers about what he had found out about the victims.

The Chief nodded. He knew that more than that had gone on and Alex was protecting him by being vague. He asked whether he should close the case as requested by Laticia.

Alex shook her head in the negative and said that the people that were murdered may had met their fate in the hands of a CIA operative, but as far as she was aware that did not give them the authority to commit murder for their convenience. She was sure what they had stumbled on had surprised Laticia and that as a good CIA boss she was going to protect the agency.

She asked that he delay closing the case for two weeks and if she and the team had not solved it by that time she would come in and ask him to shut it down for her.

He nodded and said that he would delay the closing, but the team should be careful in going after a rogue agent willing to kill ten young men to accomplish whatever he might be trying to do.

Alex agreed that they were most likely after an unstable individual and that she would make sure the team did everything by the book and did it safely.

She looked at the team and asked if they were all with her in continuing the search for the killer.

Trevor smiled and said that the case had just become more interesting, and he was eager to see how she was going to guide the team.

Bill added that ten bodies in the morgue were enough of a red of flag for him to wear his Kevlar outfit in its entirety for the rest of the time they worked on the case.

Johnnie said that he had picked off the telephone numbers of the three FBI agents and if they all wanted to listen in to the calls that he was sure would-be taking place they should all go with him to one of their favorite lunch places and participate with him in watching logs float down the river.

Trevor laughed and said that he had thought Johnnie had been standing so close to Laticia because he liked her perfume. He added that he might not want to look for logs going down the Ohio because the last time they had watched for that log he had found a dead body, and currently they had a case with all the dead bodies they needed.

8 Dissension in the Ranks

Laticia knew she had a problem and that Liam had gone off the deep end. He was on assignment to find and neutralize any foreign agents that he could identify that were operating inside the US. She was at the moment trying to get over the shock that he had executed ten men, and she had no reports from him about finding any foreign agents. She knew that he had planned to gain influence and some sort of control via the drug distribution network but that was the extent of what she knew about what he was trying to do. She had no way of contacting him. For security reasons he had always been the one to initiate contact and this time there had been silence for almost a year. She had made up her mind that she needed to report the situation to her bosses. She had to position Liam's removal in a way that would keep her and those around her from being damaged by his actions.

She had turned his laptop over to her IT support and asked them to get into it so she could find out what Liam was up to.

They had let her know that they were trying to figure a way that they could get in but so far, they had run into a solid brick wall and that they did not know how to penetrate that wall. She was not happy about their lack of success but at least that over confident black detective back in Cincinnati would have had the same problem and would know even less than she did. She was glad that she had derailed that investigation.

She looked over to where Thermon and Jason were reviewing the reports on the autopsies and asked what they were finding out. They commented that four of the deceased had been killed at the same time and then buried in a single grave. The other six had been lifted from a ravine and they had been killed within a few minutes of each other but at least a week later. That timing meant that the Cincinnati detective unit had already found the first four and were most likely at the scene when the other six had been executed.

Jason commented that it seemed that Liam had been returning to the house and when he somehow learned that the police were at the scene, he must have decided to get rid of the six. From what he could glean from the reports, the house at one time had held up to twenty-one prisoners on chains prior to the first four deceased getting shot. He added that it seemed that some of the prisoners had been chained for almost year. Jason went on to say that Liam had come up with a diabolical approach.

She commented that Liam had mentioned getting control of some parts of the drug distribution network and then using drugs to catch the spies that he had been going after. She figured that the prisoners were most likely connected with the drug business. She asked if they might have an idea of how to locate Liam.

Thermon shook his head and said that the only thing he knew about Liam was that he liked upper end places to live, and he liked to enjoy the best cuisine. He chuckled and added that the two criteria narrowed the locations to around twenty-five cities and only a few thousand top end restaurants.

Jason added that Liam also liked to attend car races and horse races and that might get them down into the hundreds of places.

If Jason could have been in New Orleans, at America's third-oldest racetrack known locally as the Fair Grounds Racecourse & Slots and watching the race, he would have been within a few yards of Liam who had come out to enjoy the race and afterwards was planning to go to enjoy a dish of Crawfish Etouffee tips served over rice. He was planning to focus on the great taste and use French bread with a garlic butter spread to soak up all the great tasting juices.

He had begun his moves on both coasts and in New Orleans. He was behind in getting started in St. Louis and he had decided to stay totally out of Chicago for the near future. He was currently focused on L.A. and on New York City where the highest concentration of spying activity was taking place.

He was satisfied with the progress he was making and planned to begin the elimination of the most active spies. He had been surprised that the most prolific spy was almost seventy and was one of his CIA bosses. His location in Washington D.C. put him out of reach there but he knew that this boss vacationed just north of downtown Miami. In one meeting he had listened to him boast of going out to where the waves had not yet started to rise and then swimming a mile each morning along the beach outside of his beachside home. The fact that he was able to afford a beach side home should have been a signal to someone inside the CIA but evidently his position had somehow insulated him from that scrutiny.

He initially had thought about a way to spike his medication, but he instead zeroed in on drowning him. It would give him so much more pleasure to pull his big boss underwater and look into his eyes as he tried to take in his last breath but instead sucked in salt water and drowned.

He gave a call to a friend back in the office and asked her to find out when the vacation was to take place. When he got that information, he made reservations in Miami. He arrived a day before the big boss's vacation and walked the beach area. He found a dive shop at one end and rented a full dive outfit with a double air tank pack. He went to where some boats were for rent and rented a boat and took it along the beach to where he planned to stage the drowning.

He figured he could anchor the boat, get in the water, and get into position where he could pull his big boss under and then return to the boat and leave before anyone knew anything had happened.

A day later in the early morning as the sun was just warming the air, he anchored his boat, got into the water, and swam to where he planned to drown the big boss. He could see him approaching and positioned himself. He was able to grab one ankle and then the second one and then pull him under. The struggle was more intense than he had expected, and he missed being able to pull him down to where he could look into the boss's eyes, but the drowning happened as otherwise planned. He was back to his boat and gone before anyone noticed a floating body.

He was sitting having a late breakfast when he heard the morning news announcing the fact that a swimmer had been found drowned.

He had a few more days before he was planning to drive back to New Orleans to plan out his next move. On the last day before leaving, he sent a text to Laticia saying, "number one spy drowned." He figured that would trigger a very intensive investigation into the drowning and most likely a search for him as well. He left the phone he had used to make the call in Miami.

The drowning had electrified the department. There were several theories about how that had happened. The coroner that had done the autopsy had listed the cause of death as drowning. He had noted that there seemed to be slight bruise marks on one of the ankles.

Laticia knew immediately that Liam had made those bruise marks. She went to her boss and suggested that a very detailed look be taken into the big boss's actions to see if there was any indication that he might have been a deep mole. That led to an argument with her boss but in the end, she prevailed, and the analysis got underway. She assigned Thermon and Jason to do that analysis and instructed them to evaluate every moment that their top boss had taken in the CIA and even to go back to his early school years.

It took them several weeks of digging but they found a pattern where meetings with a soviet counterpart went on in unrecorded meetings and that trips to Russia seemed to be lacking the details of the meetings held there. They were able to match the meetings and then actions that the Russian's took to information that had been leaked.

Jason swore when he and Thermon shared their information because Laticia made the comment that Liam had just earned a pass even thought he had killed nine people on his way to eliminating a spy within the ranks of the CIA. He shook his head and said that it did not make sense to him.

Laticia said she agreed but the single discovery meant that a huge security leak had been plugged and would never operate again.

Liam rented a car and drove back to New Orleans and started to focus on his next spy. This time he was zeroing in on a Seattle operative that was focused on disrupting a political election that could mean the control of the US senate. This operative appeared to be working for the Chinese. He really did not care which foreign country was behind the fake information that was being pushed. He was setting things up so that this individual ceased to exist. He hired a local detective to learn what the operatives habits were.

It turned out that the operative was a single, white male police officer in his mid-thirties that went to a karaoke bar, liked to sing, and drank continuously. He was doing his false messaging for the Chinese, and he was doing it because of the easy money he could make.

He arranged for Sebastian Cassidy, the distributor he had recruited and told him whose drink to spike with an overdose of Fentanyl but to make sure the overdose was just to the deadly side but not an overdone because he wanted it to look like a mistake by the person doing the drinking.

It turned out that Sebastian chose to spike several drinks and after having several spiked drinks as his target stood up to sing and took a drink, he collapsed as his heart failed.

When he learned of the death, he sent a message to Laticia, "number two, Karaoke bar, Seatle."

Laticia read the message and shared it with Jason and Thermon. She asked them to verify that the person who had died was indeed an operative that should have been targeted.

Jason commented that the two of them were doing nothing more than following dead bodies.

Thermon added that he wondered if any potential spy would be brought to trial or if dead bodies was now the normal way to handle potential spies.

9 Wisp of the Trail

Alex spent two days after the CIA folks left working with Johnnie as they tried to determine where to find the owner of the computer. Since they could not have the information officially, they were working in Johnnie's kitchen, enjoying tea and cookies as Johnnie went through hundreds of files trying to flesh out what the person that they now knew was a CIA spook named Liam was planning and why he had killed ten young men. The information on the computer verified that the first of those chained in the towers were put there almost a year before the others were killed and it seemed that a new batch was added from the east coast three months after those from the west coast and the final group was from the center of the country along the Mississippi. They shared the nine cities, Seattle, L.A., San Diego, Boston, New York, Miami, Chicago, St. Louis, New Orleans with Trey, Trevor, and Bill.

From what they could learn the abductions were based on convenience not on any specific criteria. Apparently the four who had been shot had refused to agree to work for Liam.

Trey, Bill, and Trevor were figuring out the identity of the four bodies found in a common grave.

The finger prints turned out to be key in linking the body that Trey was trying to identify to an Orson Ambrose who had been reported missing in Seatle.

A short time later Bill had a similar breakthrough with identifying a Thiago Bandello associated with a missing person's report in San Diego.

Trevor commented that once again he had been given the hardest to locate identities.

Bill laughed and said it was just because he was slow, and he should just accept the fact that he was just not as good as he and Trey.

A day later, Trevor let out a whoop as he got a hit on a Boston missing person's report.

Bill had taken up the search for the fourth victim and got a hit from a missing person report in Miami.

They all met for lunch at a restaurant that Johnnie had randomly chosen to share what they knew.

Johnnie started out the sharing by saying that he had a surprise. He asked if anyone wanted to guess what it might be.

Alex said that her guess was that he and Mary were moving in together.

Johnnie smiled and said that was partially true and checked to see if there were any more guesses.

Trevor laughed and said that his guess was that Mary was pregnant.

Johnnie laughed and said that since she was only two years younger than his seventy-seven years such a thing would make it a miracle and much more than just a surprise.

He said that he was moving into a house in Mt. Adams that was only two blocks away from where Alex lived.

He added that he had been worried about Alex riding her bike alone into work each morning and now he would be able to ride the lead all the way from her house.

Alex added that it was great that he and Mary were moving close by but now she would have to worry not only about getting shot but about him falling off his bike on the way down the steep road to the city center. She asked when the house warming party would happen.

Johnnie said that Mary would be sending out invitations.

He then said that he had a theory about what was going to happen on their case. He said that he figured the cities had been selected because of the spies or operatives that might reside there. The people that had been abducted were drug pushers and three key leaders of the drug distribution business. The leaders were strategically located on the West, East, and Center of the country. Originally the command center was to have been in the nine-tower home in Ohio but that had now changed, and a new location would have been chosen.

That location was the current critical unknown. The second unknown was who the targets happened to be.

So far Laticia's phone linkage had not yielded anything useful. He commented that if she got any communication from Liam, the target of their search, his phone would get the virus that was in her phone, and they would be able to find him.

Alex added that what they needed now was to be patient and see what Johnnie could do. She asked for him to see if he could find the money connection that Liam might have. If they could get to that source, they might be able to pinpoint his location as well.

Trevor commented that once again they were relying on an old, worn out, Vietnam War veteran for a miracle.

Johnnie laughed and invited Trevor to ride with him and Alex along the Loveland Trail to see who was worn out.

Bill quietly said, "Touche."

Alex asked Johnnie to continue to see if he could find a money trail. She added that as soon as he found it, she wanted to cut it off and see if they could flush Liam out.

She said they should go back to the office and put in their appearance and let the Chief know the progress they had made in just two days.

A day later Trevor said he had an unusual situation where a person who drowned in Miami was identified as a CIA high level employee.

Johnnie checked and said that Laticia had a text on her phone that said, "number one spy drowned." He said that he would see if he could locate the phone that had called her.

Two days later, Trey commented that he had something suspicious in Seatle.

Johnnie checked Laticia's phone again and found the message, "number two, Karaoke bar, Seatle."

He then fired up his online phone location routine.

Alex commented that Liam was now going after the spies that he had been told to apprehend but his approach seemed to be to kill them. She wondered if that was the intent of the CIA. She added that the person drowned in Miami had been identified as a CIA employee. She asked Trevor to follow up and see if he could find out what role that employee played in the organization.

She went in to the Chief's office and shared what the team had learned and let him know that Liam might now be killing spies, but it was clear to her that he preferred killing people versus bringing them in for trial.

He agreed but added that he and the team were treading on thin ice and that the CIA was a formidable organization to be challenging. He added that they were five going up against an organization that had thousands that they could leverage.

Alex agreed but added that a serial killer in any organization was bad for the country. She added that once she had him in custody, she hoped to get him in front of a judge before the CIA could step in. Then the trial would make them share more details about his role.

When she came back to the huddle room, Johnnie let them know that he thought he had the Liam's location. He said that he had managed to locate him in New Orleans.

Alex looked at the team and asked if they were ready to go to New Orleans. She and Trey would leave immediately, and the rest of the team would drive the department van down so they would have a mode of transportation that carried all their gear. She and Trey would travel light, rent a car, move into position, and wait to make any move until they all arrived. They would verify where Liam lived.

On landing in New Orleans, they rented rooms in the hotel that was within walking distance of the address that Johnnie had given them.

They then went for a walk to the location where Liam was located. There was a restaurant with outside seating where they decided to eat dinner. They relaxed at the table with a very expensive glass of Pellegrino with as slice of lemon.

Alex ordered Jambalaya that promised savory, local crab and shrimp, and vegetables mixed with rice and spices.

Trey was looking forward to his order of a crawfish, alligator combination Étouffée with roux baste onions, green peppers, and celery served over rice, with a seafood-gravy topping over it all.

They had just dug in when Alex quietly let Trey know that she was watching Liam apparently coming back from a grocery shopping trip.

They both watched as he entered the address that Johnnie had given them. Then as they watched they saw the lights on the corner top floor apartment come on.

Alex called Johnnie and congratulated him on having hit the nail on the head as to Liam's location. She asked where the three of them were in their journey. After learning that they were halfway to New Orleans and planned to make it there early in the morning Alex gave them the address of the hotel where she and Trey were staying. She added that she would rent three more rooms and expect to have breakfast with them. She suggested that each of them get some shut eye as they drove because she planned to arrest Liam the following morning.

Trevor had been listening and said that he had already gotten a three-hour nap and he would take over the driving from Bill so he could get his nap in. He chuckled and said that Johnnie seemed to have a natural sleep habit and was always needing to be awakened when it was time to take a nature break so he figured he would be good and rested when they arrived.

Johnnie came back on and said that the conversation that went on between Bill and Trevor was so boring that it put him immediately to sleep.

Alex laughed and said she was glad they were having a good trip, and she was looking forward to them getting to New Orleans where she would treat them to a couple of excellent meals.

10 Runner

The following morning Alex and Trey came down to the hotel desk and learned that Trevor, Bill, and Johnnie had checked in at three in the morning and that they planned to be down at eight. She asked where there was a good breakfast restaurant and the clerk said that the hotel was where they could get the best breakfast but there was also a corner restaurant named Maggie's that was her favorite because they had the best eggs benedict with a side of boudin sausage.

When Bill, Trevor and Johnnie got down to the lobby, they all went to Maggie's and had breakfast. Alex decided that the eggs benedict were as good as the clerk had said and she asked everyone how their choices had tasted.

Trevor commented that his order of country fried steak and eggs had been great.

Johnnie nodded and said that his buttermilk pancakes with two eggs on top and two bacon strips were great.

Bill said that his grits with a pad of melted butter topped off with syrup had him ready for action.

Alex let them know that they were only two blocks away from where Liam had his apartment. She suggested that she and Trey go up to the apartment and that Bill and Travis stay outside at the corner in case there was another way out.

She asked Johnnie to monitor the street that was on the opposite corner from where Bill and Trevor were standing.

When Liam had decided to rent the corner apartment on the third floor of the building he had done so after he had found a second way out of it that let him go across several roof tops and then climb down a fire escape to the street. He figured that if he were surprised by someone or some group of people trying to corner him, he wanted to be able to make a fast getaway. He had also installed a small camera above the door so she could see who was standing on the other side.

In spite of all the preparation he was still surprised to hear a knock on his apartment door. He looked to see who was on the other side of the door. He did not recognize either, the rather young-looking black female or the tall tough looking male with her. He, however, knew the look of people that were in the police business and figured they were looking for him. He picked up his getaway bag, his laptop computer, pulled his thumb drive from his desk top computer and went up the spiral stairs to the roof exit. He had no intentions of getting himself arrested.

He had no idea who would be trying to do so or how they had found him. He figured it might even be the CIA trying to rein him in.

He ran across to the back side of the building, jumped the very narrow passage way that existed to the next building and ran to the very back end of that building and then climbed down the fire escape to the street below. He had his car in the ground floor of that building. He went to it and drove out. He was heading toward the Pontchartrain bridge with the intent of getting out of the state. As he drove, his only regret was that he had splurged on a wide screen computer display and a desk top computer that he had to leave behind. He, however, had his laptop that had all of his work files, so he was still in good shape to continue the elimination of the countries enemies.

A few moments after, Alex again knocked on the door and when there was no answer, she picked the lock and then followed Trey as he took the lead. They both had their guns drawn but put them away once they had confirmed that the apartment was empty.

She pointed to the spiral staircase and went up and out to the roof. She walked to the edge where she was able to look down between the buildings.

She and Trey returned back to the apartment where she called Johnnie and asked him come up to the apartment with Bill and Trevor.

She asked Trey to find a rope or something else to keep the roof door from being opened while they were in the apartment.

She walked over to where a cup of coffee was sitting at the computer desk and found that it was still warm. She figured that Liam had chosen to disappear rather than open the apartment door. She wondered if he would be back.

When Johnnie came in followed by Bill and Trevor, she asked him to see what he could find on the computer.

She asked Bill and Trevor to see if there was any other useful things that might be in the apartment.

Johnnie let her know that the desk top computer did not have any of the work files he had found on the laptop that they had recovered earlier so Liam must have used the desk top computer as a way to power the large, curved screen and used a thumb drive to keep all of his working files.

Bill returned and said that Liam was a very neat person who hung his pants on pant hangers in the closet and had his shirts hung next to them and that all the hangers were equally spaced. He added that there was a sock drawer, a T shirt drawer, and a underwear drawer and that there were six of each item which meant that Liam was wearing number seven of each item. There was only one pair of gym shoes in a gym bag, so he figured his every day shoes were on Liam's feet.

Trevor came into the front room and shared that Liam had two sets of bath towels and wash clothes. He used one of the latest six bladed razors and had a small bag of floss picks and had a rotating electric tooth brush.

Trey commented that the kitchen was well equipped, and that the refrigerator was well stocked. A steak had been marinated and looked like it was what was planned for lunch along with a baked potato. It appeared that the breakfast dishes were rinsed and placed in the dishwasher. The refrigerator freezer had a gallon of pineapple sherbert that had a few scoops taken from it. He finished by saying that Liam had a bowl of fruit that had a fuji apple, a large orange, a grape fruit, and a group of white grapes in it. It was clear to him that Liam was a healthy eater and ate well.

Alex thought for a moment and decided that they should find out what they could but the opportunity to capture Liam had evaporated. She asked Bill and Trevor to see what they could learn by going to the restaurants and bars within walking distance to see if they could learn any more about Liam's habits and tastes.

She suggested they pick one of the restaurants where they would want to have lunch.

She asked Johnnie how close he was to finding Liam's bank account and if there was the possibility to cut him off.

Johnnie let her know that he was still working through Liam's encrypted computer files and that it would take a few more days to get through them.

She then asked him to send a text to Laticia letting her know Liam's New Orleans address but to wait until the team was ready to leave because the CIA might have personnel in New Orleans, and she did not want to be anywhere close when they got to the apartment.

She looked at the time and realized that it was going to be a late lunch. She decided that an early evening flight back to Cincinnati would be in order. She took the time to make three reservations back on the only direct flight that left at five thirty in the afternoon local time. That meant six thirty Cincinnati time. She decided that a late lunch was appropriate and that a snack for dinner would most likely be had on the plane.

She let Johnnie know that she had made a reservation for him so that he could get a in full day's work getting into Liam's files the next day.

She suggested that the three of them that were flying back that day, check out of the hotel and that Bill and Trevor stay, have a nice evening out and then leave early the following day and drive back to Cincinnati.

Over lunch Trevor commented that the trip to New Orleans seemed to have been a bust and that Liam was a very cagy individual.

Bill added that he was but that now he was on the run and the chances for him to slip up was increasing. He added that they were certainly dealing with a very smart individual that most probably had a twisted mind and was very dangerous.

Once they were at the airport, Alex asked Johnnie if he was able to send Laticia the text message that gave Liam's name and his New Orleans address.

Johnnie replied that he could do it just before the plane left.

Alex had been right in delaying the message until she was leaving because when Laticia received the message, she immediately called her contact in New Orleans and had a team rush to the address. They found everything the way Alex had left it and there was no trace of her presence.

Meanwhile Alex arrived in Cincinnati and when she looked up the escalator going to baggage claim, she saw Matt waiting for her and she saw Lindsey and Nolan waiting for Trey.

She let Johnnie know that he should plan on riding with her, and Matt. They would drop him off at his Apartment.

Johnnie shook his head and said that Mary had moved into their new house and had let him know that he should go there. He added that he would be down to her house in the morning to continue working through Liam's files that they supposedly did not have.

Alex said that she would open the back gate to the yard, and he should plan on entering that way so he would not have to walk the three flights of stairs up from the street in front of her house. She added that she would make a trey of cookies in the morning to make sure he had the energy to break into the critical files that enabled them to cut Liam off from access to his money.

She added that they should plan on riding down to the station after lunch to bring the Chief up to date and be there when Bill and Trevor arrived.

11 The Power of Money

Laticia wondered why Liam had sent her his New Orleans address when it seemed he had hurriedly abandoned it. She had been told that a steak that had been marinated had been left in the refrigerator as if it was to be prepared that day and the apartment looked as if it had been abandoned in a hurry. She kept wondering what would have made him do that. She put in a call to her Cincinnati contact to see if Alex Evercrest was there only to find out that she was seen getting to the police station on her bicycle at lunch time. As far as her contact knew she had not left Cincinnati. That at least satisfied her that the criminal case against Liam had been closed.

She was left wondering where Liam had gone.

At that moment Alex was talking to the Chief and letting him know about the team's failure to capture Liam in New Orleans, but they had flushed him, and he was on the run. She pointed out to the Chief that she was close to cutting him off from his money and that would make him easier to catch.

She added that she figured he had most likely fled north to St. Louis since that was within a day's drive from New Orleans. She planned to work with Johnnie to locate him again with the hopes of capturing him on her second try.

The Chief asked what she was planning to charge him with when she apprehended him.

She replied that she would bring him in on four counts of murder and then she would work with the prosecutor on how to charge him for a second set of murders in hopes that she could get him charged separately for the six individuals he had killed and dumped into the ravine. She then hoped to have his sentences be declared sequential. She said that her goal was to have him in prison for the rest of his life.

He reminded her that they were dealing with a CIA agent and that the organization would want to take control of Liam when he was in custody.

Alex said that she would work with John to have him identify a judge who would act quickly to charge Liam and set a court date so that it would be harder for the CIA to whisk him away.

She let him know that she planned to work from home with Johnnie and that she would have Bill and Trevor working from the office helping to find Liam.

The bike ride back to her house was usually the most challenging. She seldom made it all the way up the steep roads to where she lived. She most often ended up pushing her bike up the street for the last couple of blocks.

She got back just before lunch at the same time that Trey returned with some carry out Korean food. He had picked up three orders and figured there was enough variety that they could each have a little of each item and be full when they got done and there would most likely be enough for several more meals.

She helped carry the food up the three flights of steps to the house. As they got to the top she looked back down to where her bike was chained to the bike rack and commented that she loved the house but her almost vertical front yard was a challenge. She was glad that Matt had found a gardener willing to take care of it.

Trey said that the front yard was a challenge, but for him it was the fact that the person that they ended up calling the skull collector had used the third floor as his skull museum for the skulls he had harvested from the many young women he had killed.

Alex laughed and said that the third floor was why she had been able to afford to buy the house. The fact that it had made the news made the house almost impossible to sell. She had taken advantage of the opportunity and made a low-ball offer that the owner accepted. She added that since then she had converted the third floor into an art museum that she was slowly filling.

They were eating lunch when Johnnie shared that he had found that Liam had at least a half dozen bank accounts spread across the country. He had close to six million dollars to work with.

He added that her idea that he had gone to St. Louis seemed to be the right one because there was one account in St. Louis that used Lee Havers as the person on record with the bank. A check had been cashed for fifteen thousand dollars from a realtor and on the check the realtor had written that it was for a deposit on a long-term lease to a condo and it had an address on the check.

He suggested that after lunch they could all go on line with him, and they could check out the condo on the inside and the outside and get an idea of how to capture him. Meanwhile he would close all the other accounts he knew of but leave the local one open so that they would not tip Liam off.

Alex said that she wanted Bill and Travis to get themselves set up in the huddle room and they could all participate in scoping out their next attempt at capturing Liam. She commented that they needed to figure out his escape plan and path so they could set a proper trap.

Liam meanwhile was in St. Louis shopping for clothes to replace those that he had left behind in New Orleans when he had to make a hasty retreat. He had found the condo on line and had done some research about the area and learned that there was underground service through the long-established neighborhood. His research was rewarded by learning that there was one service tunnel directly under the building and there was an entrance to it in the basement. Additionally, each of the ground floor units had a set of steps down to the basement.

He had contacted the realtor and after the showing he had written him a check using his St. Louis bank. He had set up multiple identities across the countries to allow him the flexibility to disappear when necessary and the St. Louis bank was just one of several.

He was still trying to figure out who was after him. He wondered if one of the other government agencies had somehow gotten involved or if he was being hunted by his own people. It would be so ironic if they were the ones after him.

He had rented the condo because it was a nice place, but the real reason was that it was built over an old large underground utility tunnel system that was accessible from the condo's basement. He spent several days installing sound and visual sensors so he would have an underground alarm system. He did the same around the condo property. He chose to operate from his laptop versus setting up the elaborate screen system as he had done in New Orleans. He was bothered by the fact that he had to leave so quickly that he had left everything behind. He wondered if mold was growing on the steak he had prepared for a dry fry and had to abandon in the refrigerator.

Alex had followed the tour that Johnnie took them on but was bothered by the fact that it seemed that it would be too easy to capture Liam. She commented about the fact that his condo was at ground level and that the layout made capturing Liam a piece of cake. The place in New Orleans had the same feel but had been on the top floor.

She asked what made Liam choose this condo on the ground floor where capturing him seemed even easier.

Trey looked at the area surrounding the condo and noted that the condo was the newest structure in an area where the other buildings looked to be at least ninety years old. He noted that there were no power utility lines overhead. This meant that there must be an underground utility distribution system that most likely contained both power lines and sewer piping. He said that his bet was that Liam had done his research and had found that he could get access to that system from the condo that he had leased.

Alex asked Johnnie to see if he could get the drawings of the underground system.

It took Johnnie almost an hour before he let out a whoop and said that he had found the tunnel system that went under the condo building. Most of the tunnel system diagrams were in the process of being scanned into the cloud and the only parts of the tunnel system that had so far been moved into the cloud were the parts where the new construction builders paid to get it done. He pointed out that the tunnel system split three ways right at the edge of the Condo property and that there was an entrance to the tunnel from the basement of the condo. The condo had a set of stairs into the basement from all four ground floor units.

Trevor commented that in New Orleans Liam had cameras on all the approach points to his apartment. He bet that Liam would put cameras around the ground level of the condo and do the same in the tunnel system and most likely would have a strategic one in the basement.

Alex asked Johnnie if he could hack into the cameras that Liam had set up.

Johnnie said that if he could get near enough to the condo while Liam's computer was on, he would be able to, but he figured that it would take longer than normal to get through Liam's fire wall.

Bill asked if there was a chance that they could recruit one of the other condo residences to help them.

Alex said that was a good idea and asked if Johnnie could get the names and occupation of the other condo lessees.

Johnnie chuckled and said that it would cost her one oatmeal raison cookie per lessee.

It took him about an hour to go through the county property records to find out who occupied each of the units. It turned out that the unit directly above Liam's was occupied by a sixty-five-year-old DEA retiree named Chester Ramperil.

Alex decided to see if her Chicago DEA friend, Harold Zimmerman, might be able to help. She called Harold and explained the situation.

He chuckled when he understood the request. He said that picking on the CIA was even a risk for him, but he had followed her escapades long enough to know that she would most likely succeed. He warned her that afterwards, whoever her target's boss happened to be, that person might be as dangerous as the person she was going to capture.

He said that he did not know Chester, but he would give him a call and let him know that his help to capture a serial killer was needed. He was sure that Chester would be cooperative and would allow Johnnie to set up his computer in his condo.

Alex asked if by any chance he might have five people that would be available to help capture Liam because there were five escape routes and she had only four people to cover them.

Harold asked her to wait a moment. Then after a few moments he came back on and said that his team was looking forward to meeting her in St. Louis to give her a hand. He added that the fee would be that she treat he and his team to a celebration night out to enjoy St. Louis style barbecue ribs topped with the sweet brown sugar, molasses and tomato sauce that came with it.

Alex thanked him and said that she was planning to go there in a day and gave him the time and place for all of them to join up.

He said that he would see if he could recruit the St. Louis DEA group to join in and wondered if her budget could include them in the celebration.

She said that she would be pleased to include them.

12 Team Work

*H*arold let his boss know that he had volunteered to help arrest a wayward CIA agent for the murder of ten individuals and that he and his team would be going to St. Louis to do so. He added that he had contacted the DEA leader in St. Louis who had agreed to participate in the arrest.

His boss asked who he was supporting and when he heard the name he gave his approval.

Once he had clearance, he and his team caught a flight. He had arranged with his St. Louis area contact for them to provide transportation in St. Louis. He was pleased that together the two teams would field ten personnel.

He let Alex know the number of people that he had coming to back her up.

Alex was thankful that she had the kind of support that would allow her to cover all of Liam's the escape routes.

She had reserved first class seats for the entire Cincinnati team. Trevor had made a point that she was the best person that he and Bill could possibly be backing up.

She nodded and said that she had even made sure they all had some of the best rooms in a five-star hotel.

Trevor smiled and asked if she would be taking them all out for dinner.

She added that she was hosting dinner for the Chicago DEA team that evening at a top barbeque restaurant that had been recommended by the local DEA leader who had agreed to provide five of his team as backup support the next day.

Trevor said he was looking forward to St. Louis style barbeque and then asked how she planned to deploy the DEA support members.

She said that she was going to have them take positions around the exterior and down in the utility tunnels. She, Trey, Harold, and one other of his team would be on the three steps leading down into the basement from the three first floor apartments.

Johnnie would be in the condo above Liam's condo with the retired DEA agent and he would take control of all camera's and put a visual loop in so that Liam would not be able to detect or hear anything.

She smiled and said that she had saved the best position for He and Bill, who would walk up to the front door and let Liam know that he was under arrest. She said that she expected Liam to bolt and head toward the tunnel where she and Trey would take the lead to arrest him, but she suggested that he and Bill stand to the side of the front door just in case that Liam decided to take a few parting shots.

She said that once the arrest was made, she and Trey would escort Liam and go directly to the airport and fly to Cincinnati.

She looked at Trevor and asked him that if he survived would he then host the DEA to another dinner to celebrate the successful operation.

Trevor smiled and said that he had been prepared to complain about being the one to have to knock on the condo door but that hosting a celebration dinner trumped that complaint and he would be pleased to host such an event.

Alex nodded and said that she hoped everything would go as planned.

The evening dinner with Harold and his team seemed to center around tales they shared of the cases that they had previously been in together with her and Trey. They all thanked her for her gift to them of their Kevlar protective gear that had saved several of them since they received them as a gift.

They were all shocked when they learned the details of the ten young men that Liam had executed. They were all appreciative of how Alex was planning to disperse them and planning for her team to be the first line of action. They added that they would act if Liam chose an alternative for his escape route.

Early the next morning they assembled and met with the St. Louis DEA team and reviewed the arrest support scenario. Alex let them know that Johnnie would be the one that needed to get everything set before they moved into position.

Liam had a calm night and had awakened early. He planned to review his next spy take down that would happen in Boston but figured it could wait until after breakfast. He had a mini waffle maker that he had picked up while shopping and planned to use it for the first time. He also had a small bottle of pure maple syrup that he had paid an outrageous price for and planned to use on the mini waffles that he would smother them with.

After preparing them and putting them on the table he poured himself a cup of coffee and enjoyed his breakfast. He cleaned all the dishes and put the waffle maker away. Then he went in and fired up his computer.

Johnnie had gone to the condo above Liam's and had introduced himself to Sam, the retired DEA agent who took him into the kitchen and got him set up at the table. The two of them enjoyed a cup of coffee and chatted as Johnnie prepared to hack into Liam's computer.

Sam shared the fact that he had looked up Alex on the internet and found a ton about her many successful cases. He asked if Johnnie was the miracle worker that she had praised in almost all of her interviews as the reason behind her successes.

Johnnie nodded and said that she over did it a bit, but she was always making sure that her team got credit for the cases they had worked on. He shared that she had taken him off the street and had guided him to be her "miracle" worker.

When Liam turned on his computer, Johnnie put up his hand and declared that he was going into action and needed to concentrate. He sent in his hack routine and established control of all the peripheral detection devices. He then set up a continuous visual and sound loop into the entire system. Once that was done, he called Alex and let her know that it was time for everyone to get into position.

She, Trey, and Harold each went to the three first floor condos that had steps into the basement and after showing them their badges got the owner's permission to go down the stairs. Two members of Harold's DEA team moved into position at the bottom of the ladder that went down into the utility tunnel. The rest of the DEA support got into position around the building.

Bill and Trevor approached the front door and rang the doorbell.

The ringing of the doorbell and the announcement that he was under arrest and that he should open the door caused him to put three bullets through the door and then to grab his getaway bag and run toward the stairs leading down into the basement. He had not been expecting anyone. He knew that it probably was whomever had been after him in New Orleans. As he made his retreat, he wondered how he had been located so quickly. His first priority was to vacate the condo and then he would figure out who had been able to track him. He went speedily down into the basement.

The call for him to stop and kneel caught him by surprise but he reflexively pulled his weapon, but it suddenly seemed to catch fire and fly out of his hand. He looked at his hand and realized that there was no gun there. He was stunned by its absence and amazed that his hand seemed to be burning and his trigger finger was obviously broken but there was no bleeding. He looked over to where a young black woman was standing up and walking toward him. She told him that he was under arrest and to kneel down with his hands behind his head.

A tall guy was coming at him from the other side and had hand cuffs out ready to put on him and was reciting his rights.

Liam decided that he would comply and worry about getting released at a later time. He said his finger was broken and an older black guy reached up and pulled on it and popped back into place. The pull made him cry out but afterwards the pain subside. He asked why he had not waited for a paramedic to do that.

The old black dude answered that serial killers did not get medical aid from professionals. He then taped the broken trigger finger to the middle finger.

Liam knew then that he was not being arrested by any local police but some organization that had been at the house of the nine towers. He wondered how they had gotten permission to arrest him in Missouri.

Alex let him know that they had a flight to catch and that he should cooperate, or she would personally see that he did not make it.

He looked at her and asked if her shot had been an accident.

She shook her head and said that it had been the exact shot that she had planned and that she had almost the same skill with a knife for close in quiet work and she showed him her small belt knife.

He understood the reference to a knife for quiet close in work and intuitively knew she would do as she had threatened.

He decided that for the moment doing as he was told was in his best interest.

Alex led the way to the waiting car and they all drove to the airport where she had Trey take off the handcuffs and they walked into the airport and up to the first-class counter.

Liam was surprised about having his handcuffs taken off and more surprised to be flying first-class. He decided once again to relax. The worst that had happened so far was having his index finger taped to his middle finger.

Once they arrived at the Cincinnati airport, they were met by a black police officer that introduced himself as Chief Johnson and then he was introduced to a blond female as the lawyer that was going to present the charges against him to the judge who would be deciding about the next steps in his trials.

He began to realize that things were moving fast enough that he was not going to be able to utilize his CIA connections to keep himself out of jail.

It was a short ride to downtown where he was guided into a small courtroom.

The judge convened court as soon as they were all in the court and the prosecution presented two separate murder cases and six money tax evasion cases. Two IRS lawyers were there to present the six-money tax evasion cases.

He looked over at the young black female that he had learned was Alex Evercrest and the lead in tracking him down and arranging for the rapid proceedings. To his surprise his tax evasion case was to be taken up the following day.

He was sure that the way things were going he would be convicted and get six sequential five-year sentences before his cases for murder would begin. He knew that his goose was cooked unless the CIA intervened and pulled strings to get his release.

He figured that his one call would need to be to Laticia to see if she could get a lawyer to get him released.

13 The Escape

*L*aticia was furious when she found out that the Cincinnati detective was the one that had found and then arrested Liam. She was even more incensed when she found out that Liam had been charged with tax evasion and was to be sentenced the next day. She was not prepared to intervene because she was not sure how to extradite him. She also had no idea of what she was going to report to her boss.

She put a call into the head of the Cincinnati police department and insisted that he have Alex Evercrest investigated and have both her and her boss fired for breaking their promise to cease and desist as she had insisted. She was politely told to F--- off and stay out of his department's murder investigation cases.

She slammed the phone down and paced back and forth trying to figure out how she was going to message this to her bosses.

She figured she was the one most likely to get sacrificed if Liam was convicted of the murders and sent to prison. She would either be fired or sent to some backwater assignment.

She continued fuming, continued her pacing, and finally decided that she should go to Cincinnati and meet with Liam and see if he had any ideas of how to get out of the charges he faced.

Liam was in his third day of being held and taken to court on a daily basis. Each time he went he returned to his holding cell more convinced that the CIA had abandoned him, and he began to plan his escape. His hand cuffs were always put on with his hands in front of him. He was then taken to the courthouse that was across the street. One of his guards walked ahead of him and one behind. They were both armed, but it was clear to him they were junior policemen with little experience since it was always protocol to cuff a person behind his back.

He would refrain from killing them, but he would most probably need to shoot both of them. He had watched into which pocket the lead guard put the handcuff keys. He figured that the next time he was taken to court he would make his break as they went up the steps to enter the building. He counted on the guards inexperience and the fact that he had befriended them.

The next morning for the third time, he was told that he was going to the court. So far, he had been charged for not paying taxes and money laundering on his first two trips and on the third he was charged with four counts of the killing of the four drug pushers who had told him that they would not follow his orders.

He figured he was about to be charged with six counts of murder on this fourth trip. He was still upset that Laticia had not intervened. He figured it was time to make his move.

As the lead policeman reached for the court house door he turned, hit the policeman behind him in the side of the head with his fists closed and then hit the one in front of him in the same manner. Both were down and he quickly took both of their weapons, got the keys out of the pocket of the front guard, took off the cuffs and then use them to lock the wrist of the front guard to the ankle of the rear guard. He took both of their phones and threw their shoulder mikes far enough away that the two could not get to them. They were coming around as he got to the bottom of the steps and went around the corner of the building, ran to the alley, and ran behind the building toward the river.

He used one of the phones to contact his Cincinnati contact and asked him to bring him two thousand dollars in a mix of smaller bills and a passable fake ID. He ran the few blocks to the edge of the park where a few moments later, he met the contact. He thanked him for the quick response and then walked to where he saw bicycles for rent.

He walked over to and rented one for three hours. He rode along the bike path until he was near the Lunken airport.

He needed to get out of town but in a manner that would not leave a trail. However, ironically he found out that the first flight out went to St. Louis. He thought about it and figured that going there would definitely throw his pursuers off.

They would be looking for someone going anywhere but there. He bought the ticket and then walked over to the small shop where he bought a small, wheeled suitcase into which he put some snacks and then proceeded to walk through the security where he smiled when they commented that he was traveling light.

He commented that it was only a day trip, and he would be back in the morning.

When he got to St. Louis, he decided that he would go back to his condo and see if it was still being watched. He had the taxi drop him off two blocks from his condo and after making sure there was no one watching he walked up to the back door and retrieved the key that he had hidden under a flagstone and went in. He quickly packed his suit case, found the money that he had taped to the back of the kitchen sink and then checked to see if the refrigerator still had the food that he had left there. He made himself a half dozen salami sandwiches and then left the way he had come in. He walked back to where he had been dropped off and called another cab. He now had more than twenty thousand dollars which would allow him to buy a used car and then slowly make his way toward San Diego. Once there he could use the young drug dealer as he needed and then make his way out of the country.

Sam was sitting on his back porch and watched as a rather handsome man walked across the lawn and approached the back of the condo.

When he lifted the flagstone and retrieved a key, he was sure it was the downstairs neighbor who had been arrested just a few days ago.

He went in to the living room and picked up the card of the IT expert that had used his apartment the previous week and called him to let him know that the person who had been the focus of the arrest was back at his condo. He figured that it was too soon for that to be a legitimate situation.

Alex and Johnnie both got to their desks with their cups of coffee and commented that riding into work was always invigorating since it was a downhill ride almost all the way. A few moments later Trey walked in with his cup of coffee, said good morning, and sat down at his desk. Bill and Trevor followed a moment later. They both had cup of coffee in their hands and Trevor had the box of donuts and sweet rolls that had become their daily morning gift to the team.

Alex asked if everyone was planning to be in court for the fourth time that week. She expected that they would all want to be to there to hear the final charge of six counts of murder made against Liam.

They were in the middle of discussing what they planned on doing on the weekend when Trevor nodded toward the Chief's office.

Alex looked over to see Leticia knocking on the door. It was clear that she was ignoring everyone in the bull pen area.

She watched as she entered the Chief's office and then she heard the Chief raise his voice. A few moments later, Leticia exited and slammed the door behind her and left.

Alex smiled, looked into the donut box, and picked out one of the jelly filled rolls that the Chief liked, walked to his office, and knocked gently on the door. She went in and handed him the roll and asked how his morning was starting out.

He looked up and said that he hoped that Leticia was going to get taken down a few notches and sent to the back woods of the CIA assignments. He took a bite of the roll and a sip of his coffee and said that he was going to enjoy listening to Liam's fourth sentencing. He congratulated her on how she had worked with the IRS lawyers to get the money cases prosecuted first so that Liam would be behind bars when the longer murder cases would be tried.

Alex said that she had learned that from her Hawaiian lawyer friend whose targets were billionaires who he went after for not paying their legal taxes.

The Chief said that he planned to be in court to witness the last of the cases to be presented.

Alex said that she and the team were all going to walk to the court house and get the premier seats and invited him to walk along.

The Chief thanked her, but said he was going to drive down and get their just in time to listen to the indictment.

She went out and said that it was time for them to walk to the courthouse and get into their seats there.

They were the first there and sitting behind the prosecution's table where Hanna was arranging her papers. She had been the one that was taking the early lead in charging Liam with the murders he had committed.

The assigned defense attorney came in and was accompanied by Leticia who seemed to be giving him some sort of direction. It was clear that the attorney was irritated as he pointed to the seating on the observes side of the railing. He sat down, opened his briefcase, and arranged several folders on the table in front of him. He continued to ignore Leticia who continued to talk to him.

The Chief entered and asked what the holdup happened to be.

Alex let him know that the court was waiting for Liam to be brought in.

The judge entered and after a moment he made the announcement that Liam had just escaped from his police escort and was on the run.

The Chief looked at the five of them and suggested that when they capture him again, they perhaps should shoot him and save them all some time.

Alex nodded and said that he was elusive and finding him again might be a significant challenge. She suggested they get back to the station and see what they would do next.

Once back in the office they all gathered in the huddle room. Alex suggested they review what they knew and see how they could figure out where Liam might have gone.

She asked Bill and Trevor to check on flights out, Trey to check on buses leaving the area and Johnnie to check on any hits on the banks and to make sure that the St. Louis account got closed.

She then went to the Chief's office to make sure that she still had authorization to catch Liam.

Leticia was shocked to hear that Liam had escaped. She was speechless and wondering what to do next. She decided that she would see if she could get the help of the local detective unit that had so far been the ones that seemed to be able follow and capture Liam. She hoped that she had not offended the local hierarchy too much and could make amends with some financial or other support arrangements.

She went to the police station and asked to speak to the Chief of Detectives.

14 Last Chase

The Chief was explaining that the case was taking a huge chunk out of his budget, and he was getting pressure to reign in the expenditures when his support called in to say that Laticia from the CIA was trying to meet with him. He looked at Alex and told her to stay. He then said to bring Laticia in.

When Laticia came in Alex stood up and shook hands with her.

The Chief nodded and pointed to the table and they all sat down. He looked over and asked how he could be of help.

Laticia shook her head and said that she had come to apologize for her behavior and to see how she could help in bringing Liam back in. She went on to say that initially she had operated under the CIA norm of pulling all investigations into the CIA realm, but it had become clear to her that she had lost control over her operative and it was time for her to support the only organization that so far had been able to track him down and to capture him.

She commented that she knew how much effort and resources must have been put into finding him the first and second time.

Alex nodded and said that Liam was a very smart and dangerous adversary, but he was now cut off from most of the resources he had used in the past unless he somehow had access to other CIA operatives and financial resources. She added that her team had him cut off from his money and was fairly certain where he had human resources that he had positioned. But it was going to be harder for her team to find him because of their success at cutting him off from his finances.

The Chief brought the conversation back to Laticia's offer of support and told her that he had stretched his budget in bringing Liam in and now that he had escaped it would drain his budget significantly to get him back.

Laticia suggested that she foot the bill for the previous efforts and that she cover the bill for his recapture. She added that the only thing that she would want in return was to provide the defense lawyer for Liam. She added that the current one might be the one that she kept on, but she wanted him only to keep the fact that Liam was a CIA employee out of the courtroom and out of the news as much as possible. She was not going to contest the money laundering charge or the murder charges. She was only going to insist that no death penalty be imposed.

Alex said that neither of them would insist on that since it would be up to the jury to find him guilty and the Judge to impose the sentence.

She said that she was very biased since Liam had mercilessly executed ten individuals and though she found it hard to support the death penalty in most cases his situation was an exception.

Laticia said that she had come to the conclusion he needed to be brought in and incarcerated because he had killed two spies instead of capturing and bringing them in for interrogation.

Alex nodded and added that one of those spies was at the very top of the CIA and could have provided a wealth of information on how he had managed to avoid detection.

Laticia looked at her and asked how she could possibly have that information.

Alex smiled and said that she had a magician on her team. She went on to say that she knew that Laticia had two wonderful girls that were attending Brown and MIT, doing well and a stay-at-home husband who had provided them great guidance. She looked at Laticia and said that though her Cincinnati team and her were from the sleepy city of Cincinnati they had great capability and solved the cases that her Chief assigned them.

Laticia shook her head and said that she was impressed and a little taken aback. She said that she was in fact the one that was looking for help, that her career was in jeopardy because of the fact that Liam had gone rogue, she had lost control, and she needed a magicians help to save her career.

Alex said that she and her team members would figure out how to recapture Liam and make sure that he would stand trial for what he had been charged.

She welcomed Laticia to be part of the effort and when it came time for the recapture to provide additional personnel. Alex then invited her to meet the rest of the team and to be part of the planning session.

Alex led the way to the team's meeting room and signaled the rest of the team to follow. Once they were all in the room Alex asked Laticia to introduce herself and to share what she was going to contribute in the effort to recapture Liam.

Once Laticia had done that Alex asked that they go around the room and introduce themselves.

Trevor nodded and noted that Alex put him at point to deflect any bullets that might come her way, but it didn't seem fair that she was letting a new member buy her way onto the team.

There was a moment of silence as Laticia looked at Alex.

Bill broke the silence by commenting that his partner was always seeing his glass half full, and that Laticia was welcome to help recapture Liam.

Alex smiled and let Laticia know that she was experiencing what happened in every session when the team met.

She then asked what each of them had learned.

Bill said that there was no indication that Liam had left via the Cincinnati airport.

Trevor said that the only flight that had left from Lunken airport went to St. Louis.

Alex asked Trevor to see if anyone had purchased a single seat and paid cash.

Laticia commented that it did not seem to make sense for Liam to return there.

Alex nodded but added that the flight was at the right time.

Trey said that there had not been any bus tickets purchased during the time frame of the escape.

Johnnie added that no attempt to access any of the closed bank accounts had taken place.

Alex looked at the team and said that she was betting on the flight to St. Louis, but she wondered where Liam would have been able to get the money to buy the ticket.

Laticia held up her hand and said that she was going to check on something. After chatting with someone, she looked at the team and said that a local support operative had given Liam two thousand dollars in cash and a fake passport. He did not realize that Liam was on the lam.

Alex looked at the time and said that it was time to watch logs floating down the river.

Johnnie laughed and let Laticia know that it was time for lunch, and he was tasked with selecting the restaurant for lunch, but he would let her select since it was her first time with the team.

Laticia asked if there was a good barbecue rib place with a view of the river.

Johnnie nodded and said that they were going to one of his favorite places.

Everyone was taking off their plastic bibs after eating barbeque spare ribs when Johnnie's phone rang.

Trevor commented that he was either getting a call to pick up a gallon of milk and a loaf of bread from his significant other or a call from Liam to let him know where he was.

Laticia looked at Alex and asked her if Trevor was joking.

Trey laughed and said that he would not be surprised if Trevor was right because Johnnie was their case bellwether as well as their magician who always came up with some break but only after a good lunch.

Johnnie thanked the caller and looked around the table. He said that their second floor retired DEA agent who had helped them to capture Liam had called to let him know that Liam had returned to his condo, stayed for a few moments, and then left with a large suitcase and a shoulder bag.

Laticia looked at him and asked if he was kidding.

Johnnie shook his head and said that was Trevor's job. His was to find logs floating down the Ohio River.

Alex said that she and Trey were off to St. Louis for a quick trip to see what Liam had taken from the condo and to see if he had left any clues as to where he was going.

She asked Bill and Trevor to check flights out of St. Louis.

She asked Johnnie to check out used car sales within walking distance or just a few miles from the Condo.

She looked at Laticia and asked if she wanted to go to St. Louis.

Laticia asked what Alex hoped to find in St. Louis since Liam was sure to be gone.

Alex replied that she didn't have anything specific, but she wanted to know why Liam had returned to the condo and what he had left behind that might give her a clue.

Laticia said that she would welcome the chance to go.

When they got to the airport and Alex walked up to the first-class counter, Laticia asked if she was expected to pay for the first-class tickets.

Alex shook her head and said that she only expensed the cost of coach tickets, but she and Trey always traveled first class. The choice to join them was up to her.

Once they arrived in St. Louis, Alex arranged with the cab driver to take them to the condo and then asked him to wait for a short time and then take them back to the airport.

She led the way to the second-floor condo and knocked where the retired DEA agent lived.

Sam opened the door and invited them in. After greetings he led the way to his back porch and pointed out the stone where the key to the back door was hidden. Alex thanked him for having called in the fact that he had watched Liam getting into the condo.

She then led them all to the stone, lifted it, took the key, opened the back door, and entered. She asked that no one touch or move anything.

She asked Trey to check the bedroom to see if anything was missing. She then walked around the kitchen area. She saw a discarded manila envelope in the waste basket. It had two strips of tape across it as if it had been taped to something. She noted that each of the cabinets had a strip of yellow tape across the two opposing doors. That was true for all the doors except the two under the kitchen sink. She looked in the trash and saw the crumpled ball of yellow tape. She knelt down and looked under the sink. She returned to the trash can and picked up a manila envelope with tape across it.

There was one drawer that also was missing the yellow tape. She pulled it open and found a box of plastic wrap, a box of aluminum foil and a box of wax paper.

She then looked in the refrigerator. She spotted the cotto salami container that only had two slices left in it and a small bottle of mayo. She looked in the trash container again and lifted out the bread wrapper that had a heal slice left in it.

Trey came into the kitchen and said that the clothes in the closet were gone. As he recalled Liam had exactly one week's worth of clothes hanging there. He would need to review the list of things in the bedroom, but he figured that a suitcase was also missing. He added that there were no toiletries in the bathroom.

Alex asked what they had learned.

Sam said that he had seen Liam leaving with a large suitcase, so it made sense that he had it full of his clothes and also had the things from the bathroom in it.

Alex added that he had something taped to the back of the sink that had been missed when the kitchen had been searched. She figured the envelope that was in the trash would have contained a significant amount of money and perhaps a passport or two. The fact that most of the salami and loaf of bread had been used meant that he had probably made a half a dozen sandwiches and wrapped them with plastic wrap.

Trey said that Liam seemed to center on the number seven and most likely he had made seven sandwiches.

Alex nodded and said that it was time to get back to the airport so they could catch the late afternoon flight back.

On the way back to the airport she put in a call to Johnnie and asked him to see if he could find if a used car had been sold for cash anywhere close to the condo. She then called the barbeque restaurant and arranged for them to have Sam enjoy a dinner on her.

Laticia asked how what she had learned was going to help her find Liam.

Alex smiled and said that she was betting on the fact that he had made enough sandwiches so he could travel and not have to stop except for gas.

She bet on the fact that he would be trying to get out of the country. He could go north or northwest and go for Canada. Or he could go south, southwest and go for Mexico and parts farther south. She was betting on southwest and that he was headed for San Diego.

Once she got back to Cincinnati, she was going to arrange for the team to go there if she could get some sign that was where Liam was headed.

15 The End Point

Liam got out of the cab that had stopped in front of the hotel that had a flashing light advertising a thirty dollar a night stay. He paid the cabby cash and left a nice but forgettable tip. He then pulled his suitcase toward the used car lot that was a block away. As he approached the lot he saw several large SUVs. He planned to sleep in the back on his drive west. He found one that had been outfitted with cushioned side benches that folded down into a bed. It had a bent back door that refused to open but it had a space between the two front bucket seats that would allow him to get easily into the back. When he pointed out that the back doors would not open because they had been damaged, he was able to get two thousand taken off and was able to get the van for under five thousand dollars. Before agreeing to buy it, he said that he wanted to drive it to make sure it was not burning oil or had any other road problems. When he was satisfied that it would make it to San Diego, he paid for the car in cash.

He knew that the drive would be long and tedious. He set the cruise control a couple miles under the speed limit and then listened to music as he drove mindlessly across the country. He stopped at almost every rest stop to do exactly that. He was taking his time and figuring out where he was going to go and how he might continue operating. He considered himself flying blind. He had no phone, no computer, had no weapon and no way to get more cash other than what he had with him. He had two passports for two of his entities.

The plan that slowly bubbled up was to get to San Diego. Contact the drug pusher who had agreed to follow his orders and obtain a weapon and then generate some more cash by robbing him when he had the most cash. He was already facing the trials for his other murders so if he ended killing a few more people it didn't matter as long as he escaped.

He was also coming to the realization that he needed to get out of the country.

Johnnie was looking for a cash car sale from a used car lot in St. Louis somewhere in the vicinity of where Liam had his condo. He shook his head as he turned on his search routine. He had designed it to first identify a used car lot, then examine the sales of the lot and then identify the ones done in cash. He stopped after the first car lot and tuned his routine to eliminate that low ball cash sales figuring that those autos would not make a cross-country trip.

He also eliminated anything over twenty thousand dollars and then activated his routine. His routing identified four lots that met his criteria. He examined the automobiles that had been purchased and picked the used car lot where a large SUV was sold.

He called the lot, talked to the owner, and asked about the sale. He found out that the person making the purchase was a rather handsome white man most likely in his early forties who seemed to know something about cars. The lot owner said that he was also a good bargainer and had bargained the price down because the back doors were jammed shut due to damage that had happened when the SUV backed into some mailboxes. He shared the fact that the SUV had a temporary card board license tag labeled StL 1020.

Johnnie called the station and asked that they put out a BOLO to watch for but not engage a black SUV with bent rear doors.

He then realized that it was well past midnight and figured he would let Alex know the details on their ride into work in the morning.

Laticia had come to appreciate the talent she had observed as she participated in the effort to apprehend Liam. She wondered whether she could entice Alex to become a CIA operative. She figured that she would make the offer. The worse that could happen was to be turned down.

She was more concerned about capturing Liam and getting him into prison, so she could position him as an agent that had gone rogue and should spent the rest of his life in prison. She admitted to herself that she would sleep better if he got the death penalty. It was a frightening thought to her to have him alive and possibly escape and seek revenge.

She had been the one that had encouraged him to become the invisible agent that could operate on the fringes of the law. She had recognized his ability to operate in that invisible area. Early on he had been very successful at bringing in his query and turning them over for trial. She should have pulled him after a few years but had been swayed by the fact that his actions had a positive effect on her promotions. She had missed the fact that in the last couple of years he had killed many of the people he was after. She had been shocked by the ten that he was now going on trial for. In spite of that she had tried to help him get away with it by using his CIA status. It had not worked and now she was working to get him permanently put away.

Alex was tired when she got home from St. Louis. Matt met her as she came in the door and gave her a hug. He said that he had heard about the escape and her effort to get enough information to again hunt Liam down. He asked how she was feeling. She replied that she would love to bend an elbow with a glass filled with some good West Virginia hooch but was going to settle for a cup hot of green tea.

He chuckled and said that he had saved her some of her favorite Korean dishes and would love to join her with a cup of green tea.

Alex said that she would pass on a late dinner but would love to spend a few minutes sitting on the couch and just leaning on him.

The next morning when she woke up Matt was already gone. She got up, turned on the switch to the coffee machine and then went to brush her teeth and get ready to ride into work.

When she looked down the three flights to the street where her bike was chained, she saw Johnnie standing and waiting on her. She trotted carefully down the front steps and greeted him. She unchained her bike, checked that her brake pads still had enough life to make it down the hill and then followed Johnnie.

They both had their head set on and he was immediately up dating her on what he had found and done while she was making her round trip to St. Louis.

She was pleasantly surprised that he had been able to find the SUV that Liam had purchased and was pleased that he had issued the BOLO.

She said that she had a tray of cookies or brownies as a reward for his being so successful.

He replied that this time he wanted an apple or a strawberry-rhubarb pie.

Alex laughed and said that she thought his request was a great one and that she would bake several strawberry-rhubarb pies and give one to each of the team members.

When they arrived at the station and walked into the bull pen, she knew that something was up when Trevor said that he thought she should have the entire bear claw for herself.

She looked at the piece of paper that Bill was handing her. She looked at Trey and knew that it was break in the case.

She looked at the paper, gave Johnnie a hug, and said that he, as always, was the team's magician.

Trevor asked why Johnnie was getting the hug.

Alex said that though the BOLO gave her name as the person issuing it, Johnnie had been the one that had done it.

Johnnie smiled and said that he had use her name since he was not authorized to issue one.

Trevor shook his head and said that law breakers should get punished not rewarded with hugs.

Alex looked at the paper and said that the SUV had been spotted just east of Albuquerque. She asked Johnnie to call up the locations of the two cities that the two west coast victims came from. She pointed at Seatle and San Diego. She said that L.A. and San Diego were two likely cities that Liam was heading and most likely both of them.

She looked around and said that they should all plan to get to San Diego to intercept Liam before he crossed into Mexico.

Laticia came walking in and said good morning and asked why everyone had a smile on their face.

Alex suggested they all go into the meeting room where they could focus their energy on how to recapture Liam.

She said that she was betting that the drug dealer leader that Liam had recruited resided in L.A. and would be a person that Liam would seek out. Then afterwards, he would seek out the lone surviving recruit in San Diego. In both cases he would be seeking money, and weapons. She figured that money would be the primary focus since he was cut off from his normal access to cash.

She looked over to Johnnie and asked him to put a watch out to see if Liam tried to access any of his accounts.

Laticia asked how Johnnie could monitor whether Liam tried to access his accounts.

Alex replied that was why she called him a magician and that was all she would say about it.

Laticia nodded and said that she would like to offer Johnnie a position in her organization.

Johnnie gave a little laugh and asked her if she knew how to bake a strawberry-rhubarb pie.

Laticia shook her head and replied that she didn't know how to make one.

He replied that then she had no chance of getting him to leave the team he was on. He added that in Cincinnati he got cookies, brownies, pies and had a good salary and was very happy.

Laticia nodded and added that he was also on a super team. It was clear to her that she was in a room where everyone seemed to be in tune with each other. She wondered how a person created such a team.

15 The End Point

16 San Diego

*A*s he drove along, Liam realized that he would be arriving to the L.A. area during the afternoon rush hour. He decided to stop at a campsite just outside of Palm Springs. He could spend the rest of the day relaxing and planning how to get back into the swing of things.

Once he had a parking spot in the campsite, he drove to a nearby shopping center and bought a phone for less than one hundred and fifty dollars. He had the phone activated and figured he could use it to connect with the local L.A. drug leader the next day to arrange a meeting with him on his walk along the beach. He then found a store where they had a laptop that was on sale for two hundred fifty dollars. He planned to spend time during the evening to check and see if he could get access to any of his bank accounts. If that worked, he would take out as much money as possible and get it transferred to a sleeper account he had in Mexico City.

On the way back to the campground he stocked up on some snacks. He spotted a steak house and decided to splurge and have a large T bone steak, a nice glass of wine and some decadent desert of some kind before going back to the campsite.

When he got back to the campsite, he tried each of his banks. He was surprised that he could not open any of his accounts. How that had been done was a surprise to him because each account had been set up under an alias. That meant that those six identities were compromised. Without the ability to withdraw money, he was essentially broke. He was down to few hundred dollars.

He spent a few minutes recalling the phone number of his L.A. drug dealer. He was surprised that he remembered it. He put it in his phone and then dialed the number. He was surprised when the dealer answered. He took the opportunity to set up a meeting with him along the board walk for the following day. His goal was to get a loan of around twenty thousand dollars. He remembered a pawn shop where he figured he could get a cheap gun in case he needed one for the meeting.

He needed to get back on his feet so that he could set up a new operation. He decided his best bet was to get into Mexico and then figure out how to get to Brazil where he had some good connections and then finally disappear somewhere in Argentina.

It was apparent to him that some very sophisticated technology was being employed in those trying to capture him and he needed to lay low for a period of time.

Back in Cincinnati, Johnnie got excited when the monitors that he had set up to watch and see if Liam might try to get into his accounts. The monitors went off one bank after another. He let the team know what was happening and that he would soon have Liam's location. Each hit let him add more of his tracking routine until he had it installed into the computer Liam was using. Johnnie commented that Liam did not have any protection on the computer he was using so it had been easy to put his tracking routine into the computer without being flagged. He had the location where the computer was being used and said that he had one way of tracking that required the computer to be on line and a second way that required he and his computer to be within six football field's distance if the computer was off. He said that he would continue to keep his tracking routine operational at all times so that he could slowly locate where Liam happened to be.

Alex noted that Liam was in Palm Springs that was just outside of L.A., and said that the team needed to get there and then rent a van large enough to comfortably transport all of them.

Laticia had listened to Johnnie explain his capability and commented that the team had a better detection system with a fraction of the sophisticated equipment that she had at her disposal. She volunteered to provide the transportation and a driver when they got to L.A. She then said that she had access to a private jet that could take them all out to L.A. and could leave at any time Alex wanted to leave.

Bill spoke up and said that he could be ready to leave in an hour. He only needed time to pack enough clothes for a couple of days.

Everyone agreed that was sufficient time.

Alex said that would be great. She added that she figured that Liam would stop in L.A. before going south to San Diego so they would fly into L.A. and then plan on finding and following Liam as he traveled.

Liam spent the evening monitoring the news via his new computer. He was glad that his escape did not warrant national attention. He was unaware that such news had been suppressed to keep him from knowing that he was being tracked. The next morning, he drove to the beach walk where he would be meeting with Jack, the L.A. drug leader with whom he had an agreement.

He was aware that the agreement had been extracted under duress and that asking for money was not what he had wanted to do but he had done so and gotten agreement to a sum of twenty-five thousand dollars. He would have liked to get twice as much but settled for that amount. He would see how much he could get from his San Diego contact.

He arrived at the beach walk early and decided to get on line, monitor the news, and see if he was still invisible.

The flight from Cincinnati left from the Lunken airfield and the team slept all the way. Once on the ground in L.A. they drove to a remote hanger where they were met by Jason and Thermon, Laticia's two aid's and led to a large black conversion van. After loading the bags, they all got in.

Alex had saved the seat behind the driver for Johnnie who fired up his computer to begin his search for Liam.

Laticia asked where they should go.

Trevor said he wanted to see what kind of beaches L.A. had to offer.

Alex looked at the map that Johnnie had on his computer and said that they should drive north on highway one and then cross over to Vista del Mar and drive south along the coast to see if they could locate Liam.

Laticia asked why that route.

Alex said that it was the first circle that she had in mind and then they would expand outward if they struck out.

When they started their southward drive on Vista del Mar, Johnnie said that Liam had just come on line, and he would have the location in a few seconds. Johnnie located the street that led to the beach near Sante Monica Pier. He directed them to within two blocks of where the signal was originating. They pulled over and parked. Alex asked Trevor to casually walk to where the signal had originated and see if they had the right location. He should also identify the SUV and verify that it had a temporary tag.

Johnnie spoke up and said that the computer had been turned off and he was now locating the car via his computer-to-computer connection. He suggested that they wait a moment and then to casually walked by the SUV.

Trevor said that he was going to change into a short-sleeved shirt and shorts so he would look like he was headed for the beach.

Bill said that he would walk to the corner and standby in case anything transpired.

Trevor was gone for about five minutes and then returned to say that the SUV had bent back doors, had temporary tags, and gave the number on the tag. He let Johnnie know that he had sent the picture of the SUV and the tag to him.

Johnnie logged in the temporary tag and searched the St. Louis area to determine if it originated there. A few moments later he had the information and learned that the SUV had been purchased for sixteen hundred dollars that was paid in cash. It had been sold to a Lester Stock and the signature was nothing more than a squiggle.

Laticia pointed out that Stock was part of Liam's last name, so she felt that they were nine-nine percent certain to have the right SUV.

Alex suggested that while they waited for Liam to come back, they should get some carryout so they would not have to stop once they were back on the road.

Jason pointed out that they had passed a fast-food restaurant a few blocks back and suggested they go there and order lunch. They were in line to place their order when Johnnie said that Liam was on the move.

Liam had watched as Jack walked along the broad walk toward him. He picked out the two bodyguards walking in parallel out in the parking lot. He decided to step into the door of a bungalow until Jack passed by and then he would step out on his left side. When Jack came by, he stepped out and thanked him for agreeing to loan him the twenty-five thousand. He let him know that he was aware of his two body guards walking in parallel in the parking lot.

Jack said that the last time he had been kidnapped and ended up chained to the floor of a house someplace in Ohio. He said that this time he wanted to make sure that it would not happen again.

Liam said that this time he was the one that needed the help, and he would make sure that the loan was repaid with interest either in cash or in a significant in flow of drugs. He took the envelope that he was handed and put it inside of his shirt. He then exited to his left between two houses and went around back to an alley. He looked back to make sure he was not followed. He came out to where his car was parked, got in and drove away.

Jack had thought about trying to capture Liam and chaining him in one of his warehouses and perhaps beating him as well but the walk along the beach had too many witnesses. He did not want to attract attention and figured that the money was insignificant. He had bargained it down from fifty thousand to the twenty-five that he had just given to Liam. He now knew that Liam was running from something. He hoped to find out that whoever was chasing him caught him and perhaps killed him.

He called Elisa to let her know that he thought Liam was headed to San Diego.

She said that she was headed there and hoped to be on hand when Liam tried to get money from Osvaldo.

He then alerted the Puget Sound contact, and the San Diego contact to be on the watch for Liam.

He was betting on San Diego and sent one of his men down with Elisa to give Osvaldo a heads up and a hand if needed.

He had been coaching Osvaldo who was now second in command in the San Diego drug distribution effort. Osvaldo's uncle was the number one and had welcomed getting connected with the L.A. organization since it helped him overcome some of the smaller local Mexican gangs that competed with him. The flexibility to float any extra drugs from one city to the other improved the distribution fluidity and made managing the cash flow easier. It was a win-win for the two organizations.

Johnnie was constantly giving an update on location and Jason, who was now doing the driving, was keeping up with Liam. He found it hard to keep the right distance behind so they would not be spotted but managed not to lose Liam as they drove south on the very busy interstate five. Jason was keeping track of Liam's car visually and followed him off the interstate to a large truck stop where Liam gassed up and then walked into the station to a Cheeky Fela fast food restaurant.

Alex suggested they gas up and go next door to the competing fast food and get a late lunch. Everybody was back in the van and were watching when Liam returned and got in his SUV.

Laticia asked when Alex planned to capture Liam.

Alex said that she hoped to utilize Laticia's San Diego team so they would have overwhelming superiority when she closed the trap. She hoped that wherever Liam chose to spend the night was conducive to his capture.

17 Payback

Osvaldo received the call from Jack letting him know that Liam had stopped and received twenty-five thousand dollars of a fifty thousand dollars ask and that he was probably on his way to San Diego and might try to get more from him. He in turn let his uncle know of the situation. Osvaldo was hoping that he would be contacted. He had no intentions of giving Liam any money, but he had other plans for him.

His uncle slammed his hand on the desk where he was sitting and told him that Liam was going to pay for having killed his favorite nephew, Thiago. He described how he was going to shoot him through both knees, then his feet, then his shoulders and finally he would shoot him between his eyes.

He was silent for a moment then shook his head and described another scenario where he would first nail his feet to the floor and his hands to the wall before shooting nails from a nail gun all over his body and then finishing him off by shooting a nail through each eye to kill him. He nodded and said that he would use a nail gun. He made a call and gave instructions on how to prepare the warehouse for a special occasion.

The two of them were sitting in the warehouse office when Elisa and one of Jack's men arrived. They said they were there to make sure that Liam got what he deserved and that they were there to take part in whatever retribution that might be planned.

Liam got to San Diego and found a motel that had a vacancy sign flashing out front. He parked and went in and got a room. He had been working on remembering the phone number that he had listed for the one survivor from San Diego. When he recalled Osvaldo, the phone number popped into his mind. He could not remember Osvaldo's last name but that did not matter, what mattered was being able to call him and let him know that he wanted to meet, and that Osvaldo should bring fifty-thousand dollars with him.

Osvaldo was still in the warehouse office sharing a drink with everyone when he answered the call from Liam. He agreed to fork over fifty-thousand dollars, but that Liam needed to come to him since turning over that much cash was going to be a major effort.

Liam agreed but warned him that he would be armed and would not hesitate to shoot if it was a trap.

Osvaldo replied that he had learned his lesson and personally would not take any action against him.

Once the call was over, his Uncle laughed and said that Osvaldo should enjoy watching. Elisa said that she wanted to participate and fire the nail gun into Liam's private parts.

Johnnie had managed to keep track of Liam because he had hacked into the computer but other than location he had no other way of knowing what was going on. Suddenly he said that Liam was on the move. Everyone had been sitting debating whether they should get a room for the night, but Alex had decided that they should wait to make sure that Liam was staying in for the night.

Trevor gave her a hard time about missing his dinner time.

Alex reached into her bag and handed out an energy bar to everyone in the van.

Suddenly Thermon pointed to where Liam had parked and said that Liam was leaving the hotel. He started the van and followed.

They drove into a warehouse industrial area and watched as Liam pulled up to a warehouse door and honked. The door rolled up and open and once the SUV drove in it rolled back down.

Thermon parked on the street, and everyone got out. Alex reminded everyone to put on their Kevlar outfits including their gloves and head gear.

Laticia commented that her team had the standard bullet proof vests and that she was impressed with what the Cincinnati detective unit gave to its people.

Bill shook his head and said that their protective suits were gifted by Alex, and they had saved each one of them multiple times. They were all believers in their gear.

Alex noted that the warehouse was twenty bays long and that the car had entered in about the middle. She suggested that Bill and Trevor lead the way down the front and Thermon and Jason follow them. She, Trey, Johnnie, and Laticia would go down the back side and see if they could find a way in.

Trevor pointed out that there were regular entrance doors by each one of the roll up truck doors and that they would try the ones closest to where the SUV had entered.

Laticia commented that she had put in a call to the San Diego folks and had learned that the San Diego team had been prepared to join them the following day and that it would take them several hours to get to where they were currently located. She had told them to get prepared just in case she called for help.

Alex led the way around the back. She saw that the back was a duplicate of the front and figured that trucks could drive in one side get loaded or unloaded and then drive straight out the back. She counted the doors and pointed to the one she thought would be where the SUV would drive out.

Inside Osvaldo greeted Liam and said he was pleased to see him. He did not say why he was pleased until Liam was near him, and his uncle's men jumped out and put guns to Liam's head and disarmed him. Two of them literally picked him up by the arms and carried him into the room where his uncle was waiting for him with the automatic heavy duty nail gun.

Liam was pushed down into the chair and his uncle nailed his hands to the arm rest, then had his feet positioned and nailed them to the floor.

Liam screamed continuously as his hands were nailed to the chair and his feet were nailed to the floor.

His uncle then explained that he was going to feed him as much money as he could stuff down his throat as he alternately continued to put nails in every part of his body.

He then handed Elisa the nail gun.

She asked if Liam remembered her.

He nodded his head and said that he hoped that she did not hold a grudge.

She laughed and said that she did not hold grudges but focused on getting even and then she shot a series of nails between Liam's legs.

Liam continued his screaming. It was hard for him to think. He needed to somehow get the nail gun to stop. His mouth was forced open, and a wad of bills were stuffed in.

Osvaldo stood to the side and commented that he was going to keep his promise and not take any action against him but his father and uncle of the person he had shot back in Ohio was going to keep shooting nails into him until he begged to die.

Alex was counting the doors as they walked along the back when she said she thought she heard someone screaming. She picked up the pace and when she got to the door that she figured was the right one, she tried to open it but found it locked. She took out her kit and after a few tries she managed to pick the lock.

It was dark inside and almost impossible to see anything. She led the way toward where the screams were coming from.

Trevor led the way along the front of the warehouse and opened the door nearest where the SUV had entered. Once inside he cautiously moved towards where it was parked. The four of them had heard the screams and had their weapons at the ready.

All was quiet as Johnnie led the way toward the location of where he instinctively knew the screams had originated.

He spotted movement on the other side of where the SUV was parked. He flashed his light, got a response, and knew that Trevor and Bill were approaching from the other side. There was a door lit by a small overhead light to his right.

They approached and Johnnie knelt down and tried the door that opened inward into a well-lit room that was empty except for Liam who was riddled by nails and most certainly dead since he had a nail through each eye.

Alex slowly approached Liam and realized that he had hundreds of nails in his body. There were four nails in his skull. He had a nail through each eye and one nail in each temple. She wondered which of the four nails had ended Liam's life.

A few moments before, one of Osvaldo's men had come in and said that there were eight people that had entered the warehouse and were coming toward where they were located. His uncle said that he was done and fired his last four nails and pointed to the exit to the roof and said that they should all go quietly and leave their trophy to be discovered by whoever was coming. He was sure it was not any of his competitors so it must be the law and he did not need to have a run in with them over some worthless scum that was now dead. He added that he was feeling good, and that he was treating everyone to a round of drinks. They should all go and celebrate the passing of a person who did not deserve to live.

Laticia stopped when she got into the room. She placed a call to the San Diego team and said that she needed them to come and clean a site and make what they found disappear. She did not want the local law or the media to find out about the situation. She wanted it to be a very thorough job and that nothing should be written, and everything needed to be disappeared. She then detailed how to get to where they were located.

She looked at Alex and asked her what she planned to do.

Alex shook her head, replied that her case was closed, and she was ready to return to Cincinnati and formally write up the paperwork to close it.

She added that Liam had killed the wrong person when he had killed the individual from San Diego, and he had underestimated the type of revenge that would be implemented.

She then shared that she had been asked whether she thought Liam should get the death penalty and she had said that he certainly deserved it though she was usually against it. However, at that time, in her heart she felt he deserved it.

Seeing what had happened to him she figured that some being had agreed with her and had delivered a fate beyond what she could ever have imagined. The thing that bothered her was that she felt that how Liam had died was appropriate for the deaths that he had so negligently handed out.

Trevor shook his head and said that he felt the same way and it did not bother him.

Johnnie said. "A man reaps what he sows. The one who sows to please his sinful nature, from that nature will reap destruction. Let us not become weary in doing good, for at the proper time we will reap a harvest if we do not give up

18 Case Closed

*A*lex was sitting with Tracy, her analyst, and sharing the fact that her lack of remorse for how the person who she was after had died was having a negative effect on her. She commented that the case where she had hunted down and killed many of the members of several groups who kidnaped, raped, and then killed women had not affected her like this most recent case. The case where she had hunted down a woman who had killed her mother and then had become a black widow that killed the men she had sex with had not affected her like this most recent case. The case where she had had almost lost her partner and then had followed a trail of drug dealing bosses who she eliminated had not affected her like this most recent case. Even the case where she was the target of a racist maniac who she ended up following into the woods of Mississippi killing had not affected her as much as this most recent case.

Tracy asked what made this current case so different.

Alex thought for a moment and commented that in the other cases she had to deal with the fact that she had killed multiple people or had been the target of killers trying to kill her. She always tried to arrest the people she was after, but she never hesitated to shoot if they tried to kill her. She said what was different in this case was that she felt no remorse for the fashion of death that the person she was after had suffered but instead that she thought that he got what he deserved.

She mentioned that Johnnie had quoted a biblical verse about reaping what one sows. She not only agreed with it but wondered if it was enough and would there have been an even more cruel way to inflict death. It was this last thought that bothered her.

Tracy asked what the perpetrator had done to make her think that.

Alex said that he had executed ten young men and dumped six of them in a ravine because he had decided they were useless baggage. She thought for a moment and added that perhaps she had wanted him to face the jury, then listen to the guilty verdict and then spend the rest of his life behind bars thinking about the nature of his crime. She looked to Tracy and said that he had suffered an agonizing and painful death, but she added that it had been over too fast and instead of regretting having killed the young men, the moments before his death was focused on his pain, it was focused on himself.

Tracy nodded and said that she found it admirable that what Alex was describing was not the need for revenge but the need for the guilty person to spend time contemplating the error of their ways. She suggested that Alex share her perspective with the rest of the team. She let Alex know that the rest of the team had scheduled sessions with her so she might have another perspective once she had experienced those sessions but for the time being she suggested that Alex should not worry about the lack of remorse but focus on the good feelings she had about the friends around her.

Alex thanked Tracy and went back to where the team was sitting around their desks.

Travis looked at her and asked if her session with Tracy had done any good or was, she just as crazy as before.

Alex smiled and just replied, "I love you too" and sat down. She shook her head and said that as horrible as the sight had been of the way Liam had died, she had found it hard for her to feel sorry for him, but she felt angrier that he would not get to think about what he had done. She said that she felt he had gotten off easy.

Bill nodded and said that he understood her feelings and that for Liam it was over but for the team they would live knowing that ten families would wonder what had happened to their sons. He said he had similar feelings about Liam having gotten off easy.

Johnnie pointed to the Chief's office where Tracy was just closing the door and commented that whatever Alex had just shared with her had caused Tracy to meet with the Chief.

Not too long after Tracy left, the Chief signaled for all of them to come to his office.

After they were all seated at the table he asked if all the closing paperwork had been submitted. He asked each of them to give a quick summary of their perspective of the case. They all had very similar points about the case and how its closure had been very different than they had expected.

The Chief then said that he had a few additional pieces of information that he had to share. Each of the ten victims had been identified and their next of kin would be notified. The IRS had collected the taxes on the Liam's accounts. He added that the remainder of the money had been put into a fund that had been set up to help needy kids. He went on to share that a report from Laticia complemented all of them for the professionalism, skill, and bravery that they had shown in the field.

She recommend that each have the entry put into their records that the CIA thanked them for the help in neutralizing a roque CIA agent.

He went on to share that the department received compensation for the time and effort that the team had spent on the case as well.

He smiled and said that the department was extremely happy with the fact that the budget was back in balance, and he would be able to gainfully employ them on the next case.

He looked around the table and said that he felt so good about everything that he was inviting them to a Sunday grill out at his place.

The End

Preview of: Abandoned

1 A Life Worth Escaping

*B*ento thought back over his life and realized that it had been one spent at the bottom of Brazilian society. His parents tried to give he and his eight brothers and sisters as good of a life as they could. Theirs was a hard life being servers of the wealthier. His mother was a maid to several families that were not necessarily rich, but they were well enough off to have a part time maid. His father was a laborer that was often unemployed and looked for day labor. They both worked hard to keep a roof over their head and keep everyone clothed and fed. They were firm but they never beat any of them.

He always figured their big mistake was having eight kids. He was the youngest. He got all the hand me downs in clothing. He was also often the one that got the least food when times were extra hard.

His tumbles with his brothers and sisters hardened him and he learned to get what he needed. He knew it had definitely shaped how he assessed those that he mixed with.

His schooling was spotty, but he did get through Ensino Médio, (secondary education). He was not a great student, and he did not like the school environment.

Then after getting out of school the reality of his situation hit him. No matter how hard he tried, he couldn't find a meaningful full-time job. To no avail he tried every means possible to land a job that paid well enough that he could move away from his parents and live on his own.

Then one of his school friends got him to become a "distributor" which was a fancy name for becoming a drug dealer. It turned out he was very good at being a distributor and was soon making enough money that he was able to enjoy some of the things in life that he had always seen others enjoying such as a day on the beach, eating at a restaurant, even dating. This made him become even better at distributing. He was soon rising in the ranks of the local drug ring. He was called in to meet with the two big bosses who congratulated him on his good sales and gave him a bigger territory to manage.

He was able to move into a much better neighborhood and into a decent apartment. Decent in that it was at least a step up from what he had been living in.

Not long after he met Janaina at a small local diner. He asked her out and soon they were dating on a regular basis. He was pleased that she was attracted to him. She had a knockout figure and her tanned white skin, black hair set her apart from other young women he had his eyes on.

It helped his ego that she said that he was the best-looking guy that she had ever thought of going out with. It was about a year later that he proposed.

His mother suggested he bring Janaina to dinner so that she and his dad could meet her.

That dinner turned out to be a catastrophe.

His mother was surprised and upset that Janaina was white. She let him know that she did not approve and didn't want mulatto or a pardos for a grandchild.

His father didn't say anything, but he did not come to his defense either.

It was clear that he was not going to get the approval of his parents, but he was not going to change his mind because they objected.

When he got married, his brothers and sisters attended his small wedding but neither of his parents showed up. Janaina had no relatives and there were only a few of her friends at the wedding. Almost all of the distributors that he managed were in attendance, which made him feel good since it showed him that he was doing a good job with them. He also realized that he truly was a drug dealer.

He was making enough that he could afford a small loft apartment, some new furniture and food was no longer an issue for him. It seemed that the two of them were headed into a good life.

Less than a year later, Janaina let him know that the was going to be a father.

This was good news, but it also bothered him.

Good news in that he wanted to be a father.

It bothered him that his child would someday find out that he was a drug dealer. He had become one of the top distributors and the big boss had put him in charge of several other distributors. His job was to make sure that those working for him gave him the right amount of money and that they kept only the cut they had agreed to. He was very good at making sure that those working for him were "honest."

Since all the sales money came to him and he took it into the office, he was often in possession of more money than most people made in a year.

The day came when he rushed Janaina to the hospital and waited outside of the delivery room. They had spent many hours looking at baby names and had selected one for a boy and one for a girl. It would either be Afonso if a boy or Aurea if a girl.

The nurse who came out let him know that he had a beautiful baby girl and that he could see her through the window in the nursery. He stood looking through the glass and what he though was the best-looking baby in the nursery.

He waited until she as carried out and followed the nurse to the room Janaina was in. He gave her a hug and then held Aurea for the first time. He though his heart was going to break because he was so happy.

A few days later, Aurea came home with Janaina. A home that now had a happy but worried father. He decided that he had to find a better life for his family than the one he had grown up in. He dutifully saved as much money as he could while he looked around for a way to escape his current role managing half a dozen distributors.

He was aware that he couldn't just tell his bosses that he was getting out of the distribution business. He was at a level where he had seen what happened to those that cheated or tried to move to another organization. Those people were somewhere pushing up grass and flowers. They could neither quit nor change allegiances. He did not see a way that he could possibly escape his current situation.

He was watching the news about a shooting in Cincinnati, Ohio and listened as a black female detective was being asked about the fact that she had solved a fifteen-year-old cold case and had saved the person who was now a young woman that had two children by her kidnapper. The story seemed to spark and light a fire within him. He had no idea where Cincinnati was located other than in the US, but he now had a goal. He would leave Brazil and go to Cincinnati. He would go where a black woman was seen as a heroine.

He found out where Cincinnati was located. He then found out how much it would cost to get there.

His goal to save the astronomical amount and to get visas took him much longer than he anticipated. The time turned into years and his role in the drug distribution business continued to flourish.

Aurea's sixth birthday was the catalyst that finally and very loudly fired the starting gun. During the party she said that she wanted to be just like him.

"Just like him." "Just like him." "Just like him." Kept going through his mind. He didn't want any of his children to ever be just like him at least not the person that he currently had become.

He got the tourist visas for the US. He then skipped the payment on his apartment and arranged with Janaina to leave the country. He was short on the amount of money to pay for the airline tickets, but he had an upcoming money collection round that would give him what he needed and enough money to live for a few months in the US.

He figured that the amount of money did not matter. If he took it his fate would be the same no matter the amount. He made his collection rounds and headed straight to the airport where Janaina and Aurea were waiting for him.

He was constantly looking out for anyone that might be looking for him.

He was a wreck by the time that they got on the plane. He knew that he would be hunted but once on the plane he was able to relax and when the plane finally took off, he felt that he had made his escape.

He doubted that anyone would learn where he had gone, and he was going far enough away that he figured no one would be sent after him.

The plane laned in Miami where they went through customs before going on to Cincinnati on a regional flight.

He was surprised that they landed in Kentucky at the Cincinnati International Airport. He got a ride to the hotel that he had rented that was on the western side of the city. He rented a room with two beds, for two weeks. On the same day as his arrival, he walked across to the other side of eighth street and got two jobs. One was as a short order cook and the other was managing the cash register at a gas station. He was surprised at how easy getting started was for him. He wondered about how long it would take to work his way up to some bigger, better paying jobs.

He asked Janaina to find as inexpensive an apartment to rent as possible and to get Aurea enrolled in school.

He was surprised at how quickly Janaina found a furnished two-bedroom apartment that was over a small restaurant in the downtown area. It was very basic and had mostly older furniture and appliances.

It was within walking distance to his two current jobs and the school where Aurea would go. This would allow him to continue working where he was until he could figure out how to get some better job or jobs.

He was impressed when Aurea took the school's entrance test and got placed one level above what he and Janaina expected. She had done so well that the principal commented that she was being placed one level above that was normal for her age, because her math and reading scores were so high that it was warranted. The principal also said that her verbal English skills were a little rough but good enough that she would have no problems.

Janaina was also very happy about everything. She had Aurea enrolled in school and she had talked herself into a part time job at the restaurant that was just below the apartment.

He was relieved that with their three incomes, they would be able to pay the rent, have enough money to buy food and be able to save for a rainy day. He figured that in a few months they would be in good financial shape.

The year flew by. There was little time for anything but work and more work. He made it a point that whenever he could the three of them did something together. They often went to the riverfront and enjoyed the free games that were available there and to have a picnic on the lawn.

On one occasion he splurged and rented a segway so that Aurea could experience riding it. They had a great time riding it together for a short time, but he was afraid that they might have a wreck.

During the summer they attended several free outdoor concerts where they sat on the hillside and enjoyed a picnic. Then during the winter, they made it to the ice-skating rink and all of them tried their luck on the ice.

Aurea was the one that seemed to be a natural. He and Janaina took off their skates and watched Aurea go around the rink. They held hands and smiled as they watched their beautiful daughter laughing and enjoying herself.

In the spring they walked across the Purple People's Bridge and when they got to the other side, he bought Aurea a bratwurst that they all ended up sharing.

He and Janaina agreed that their move to Cincinnati was the best decision they could have made.

Aurea spent almost all her extra hours at the main public library. Janaina had enrolled her in an after-school program that featured a variety of supervised activities. This allowed her to work at the restaurant while Aurea enjoyed herself in a safe environment.

It was a good year and it seemed that life for him and his family was on an upward path.

He was standing at the grill flipping a series of burgers when the cashier said that there was a rather tough looking dude at the counter asking to talk to him. He walked out and almost fainted when he saw Cristiano standing on the other side of the counter. He knew that Christiano was the mean partner of the drug distribution ring in Sao Paulo and if he was in Cincinnati, it meant trouble. He almost turned and ran but instead he faced Cristiano as if he had no fear when in fact, he was about to wet himself.

Cristiano spoke to him in Portuguese and asked him if he had the money that he had taken from his operation.

If the situation hadn't been so serious Bento would have laughed. He had spent the money and there was no money other than the little he and Janaina had been saving. That amount was a far cry from the money he had taken from the drug business. He knew if Christiano had personally made the trip he was there to make a point and to make an example of what happened when someone crossed the organization.

Christiano shook his head and smiled as he said that if he got his money back, he would only kill him but if that didn't happen, he would take some of that payment from Janaina before he killed her.

He figured that there was no money, so he said that he was also planning to cut out his tongue and cut off his ears, take them back to Sao Paulo and hang them behind the bar with a sign that declared that thieves were always caught and rewarded for their actions.

He asked what Bento had to say while he still had a tongue.

Bento stood silently as he thought about what he had to do.

Christiano nodded and said that he would be waiting out in the parking lot and that Bento should make it easy on himself. If he came out to the parking lot, he would kill him before cutting out his tongue.

Bento nodded and put up his hand and then turned and went back into the kitchen area. He did not stop at the grill but headed straight out the back door. He ran all the way back to the apartment.

Janaina had just returned from school with Aurea. She was surprised to see him and when she understood that they had been found she was as afraid as he was. She knew that they had to make a run for it, and she knew that they had to find a safe place to leave Aurea.

She said that they needed to get out of the apartment, and they needed to get Aurea to a safe place.

He convinced her that they would be safe until the next day.

Janaina said that she knew where they had to take Aurea and they had to do it very early the next morning.

A few hours before sunrise they all left the apartment with all the food they could carry and with Aurea's clothes, the few toys she had and a family picture of the three of them together in the park. It all fit in a large black plastic bag.

Aurea was confused about what was happening. She kept asking why they were walking across town in the dark.

Janaina led the way and crossed on the walking bridge that led to Mt. Adams. She was taking her to the only place she felt that Aurea would be safe. She did not know how she was going to be able to leave her there by herself, but she knew that she had to leave her and that she and Bento needed to try to make their escape afterwards.

She stood and looked up the three long series of steps that led to the house. She took Aurea up and had her sit on the porch swing with all her things. She then gave her a hug and let her know that she was loved but she had to stay here where she would be safe.

Bento knelt down and gave her a hug and repeated the fact that she was loved. He handed her a large envelope and said that she should give it to the lady that would come out on the porch later in the morning.

He looked at Janaina and said she should stay.

Janaina shook her head and said that Christiano had come for her as well. Back in Brazil he had often threatened to have her when she was through with her lover. He would just find her later, so she was going as well.

They both descended the steep steps and walked back to the downtown area.

They asked each other where they should go. They came to the realization that there was no place to run to.

They decided to have breakfast at the restaurant where Janaina worked and wait for the inevitable.

They had just finished their breakfast when Christiano walked in. He looked around and asked if he could join them at their table. He smiled and asked if they were ready for a ride out to the countryside. He then asked where their lovely daughter was and when he got no answer he simply said "good" I have no interest in her.

He stood up and said they should follow him.

The owner came out and asked if everything was OK.

Janaina smiled, said that she appreciated his concern, but everything was fine as she gave him a hug and then followed Christiano out to the car.

The owner followed but stayed in the doorway. He took a picture of the license plate and stepped back inside. He figured he had enough of his own problems and didn't need to get involved in his employee's problems. He suspected that they were in the country illegally.

Christiano instructed her to sit in the back and let her know that he had a gun that would be aiming at Bento if she tried anything.

He then got on seventy-one, drove several exits past King's Island before exiting and driving through the farm country. Then at a sign that declared that the road was to be used by only authorized personnel, he turned and went into the forest. He hoped that it would not be used while he was having the graves dug and he was covering them up.

He stopped the car and instructed the two of them to get out and walk around to the front of the car. He screwed on a silencer as he walked around to meet them.

Janaina saw what he was doing and as fast as she could she ran towards him. She hoped to knock him down so that Bento could kill him.

Bento realized what she was doing and rushed after her.

Christiano barely had time to finish putting on the silencer before he was hit and knocked back a step by Janaina. He shook his head and said "muito ruim para você" and shot her between the eyes.

Bento thought he was going to get a chance at taking Christiano down when he felt the bullets hit him in the chest. He gave Christiano a finger and then the world went black.

Christiano shook his head when realized that he would need to dig the graves to bury the two. He had planned to have the two dig their own graves.

He put on his rubber gloves, cut off Bento's ears, his tongue and put them into a plastic bag between aluminum foil and sealed it. He dropped the bag into a US priority mail envelope that he would mail when he got to the airport.

He found a place where a natural dip in the land provided some initial depth and then he went to work. He decided that one grave would be sufficient. He put them both in, covered the grave, made sure there was a rock layer across the top and then put old leaves and some tree branches over all of it. He stepped back and decided that it would never be found.

Not far from the grave he found a large flat rock and put the gun under it. It was a gun that he had paid for in cash on the street and would never be traced to him even if it was found.

He then left but before reaching the highway, he threw the shovel into the ditch.

He felt justified and successful as he drove back to the airport.

A short time later, he drove into the car rental and a few moments after that he rode the shuttle back to the terminal. Once inside he dropped his envelope into the mailbox then walked up to the check-in counter.

He was not flying directly back to Brazil but was flying west to visit the Grand Canyon and then walk out on the see through walkway that would give him a look down into the canyon. He also planned to visit Bryce canyon and enjoy a hike before flying to Mexico City where he would spend several days and then fly back to Sao Paulo.

He figured that he might as well mix some pleasure with business. The business had been quickly done and the pleasure, though brief was what he was on his way to do.

He looked forward to getting back to Sao Paulo and a relaxing time there. He hoped that the mail would get there before him.

2 The Package on the Porch

Matt was still out with the EMT team, but Alex figured he would be arriving shortly. She was ready to prepare breakfast and was waiting until he arrived. She had invited Johnnie to join them and afterwards they would take their normal ride into work.

She hoped that Matt had an easy night, but she knew that was seldom the case. He told her the time right after the closing of the bars usually was peak time for his team to make several runs from some accident to the nearest hospital.

The doorbell rang and she figured that Johnnie had arrived. She went to the door and opened it.

She was not surprised to see Johnnie, but he was holding a bulging black bag in one hand and had his other hand on the shoulder of a beautiful, auburn-haired young girl who looked to be frightened.

He commented that she had been sitting on the porch swing and said that her mother and father had dropped her off where she would be safe.

Alex knelt down and asked the young girl her name and learned that it was Aurea. She then asked Aurea why her parents had left her on the porch.

"Because they wanted me kept safe and you are the only one, they trusted to keep me safe," Aurea quietly replied. She gave the envelope she had in her hand to Alex and said that her mother said that it was for her.

Alex accepted the envelope looked in it expecting to find a note and was surprised that it did have a note, but it was also filled with one-hundred-dollar bills. She looked up at Johnnie and asked what was in the black bag.

He put it down, looked into it and replied that it looked like clothes and a few other odd and ends.

Alex asked Aurea to follow her and as she led the way to the kitchen she asked if Aurea would like to have some breakfast.

She had Johnnie put the bag down just outside of the kitchen door.

She handed the envelope to Johnnie and asked him to count the amount of money in it.

She offered Aurea some eggs, pancakes, and a lot of syrup.

That got a smile from Aurea.

Alex asked when her parents would be back to pick her up.

Johnnie chuckled and said that given what was in the bag and the money in the envelope he figured it might be a long time.

Alex was trying to figure out what to do when Matt walked in from the backyard.

He smiled and said that he wasn't expecting company for breakfast.

Alex gave him a hug and introduced Aurea who had been dropped off on their front porch for safe keeping.

Alex asked him to sit down, and she would get him his breakfast.

Matt sat down and started a conversation with Aurea.

Alex knew from past experience that kids normally liked Matt and Matt had a natural way of talking to them.

He first asked her for her mother's and father's name. He asked where she was from and learned that they had come from Sao Paulo. He learned that they had been in Cincinnati almost a year.

He soon knew what school she was attending and the names of her teachers. He learned that her favorite place was the library where she normally spent her after school time. She liked the River Front Park because there were free games. He found out the address where she and her parents lived.

Alex kept quiet as she wrote down what she was hearing.

Johnnie joined her and asked what she was planning to do about the situation.

She replied that she was going to take the day off to find out what was going on.

Johnnie offered to help and suggested that he call Mary and ask her to come over to watch Aurea while the two of them investigated the situation. He added that Matt needed to get to bed and get some rest since he had been out the entire night.

Alex thought for a minute and then said that if Mary didn't mind her help would be greatly appreciated.

Johnnie gave a little laugh and commented that Mary would most likely love to do it. He walked out into the backyard and made a call. A short time later he walked back in with Mary.

Matt finished his breakfast and thanked Aurea for sharing her time with him. He looked at Alex and asked if she had the situation covered and smiled when he saw her mouth a thank you to him. He nodded and said he was going to take a shower and then get a good night's sleep.

Aurea asked who was going to take her to school.

This was something that Alex had not thought about.

Mary sat down at the table and asked where she went to school. She said that she would take her and asked when she had to be there.

Mary looked at Alex and asked if she had the right idea of why she had been called.

Alex nodded and said that if Mary could accompany Aurea and find out her routine it would be a great help. She added that all expenses would be paid. She also asked if she could get one of the guest bedrooms ready for Aurea.

Johnnie pointed to the black bag and said that he figured everything that she had was in the bag.

Mary opened the black bag, looked into it, and let out a whistle. She reached in and took out a framed picture of Aurea and her parents. She handed it to Johnnie and said the picture might come in handy.

Alex walked out of the kitchen to the back porch and called the Chief. She informed him of the situation and let him know that she was going to treat the situation like a case, but she was going to take the day off to do so.

He said that she did not need to use her vacation and that he wanted her to come in and that he wanted Trey to join her in her investigation. He made the point that parents dropping off their child on a strangers porch was very unusual and he figured the situation merited handling it like an actual case that needed to be investigated.

She agreed to come into the office with Johnnie and to get things organized.

When she went back into the kitchen, Johnnie asked her if she planned to eat breakfast.

She shook her head and said that the two of them should plan to ride to work and figure out what the next step would be.

She went to the drawer in the kitchen and took out several hundred dollars and gave it to Mary and told her to use a taxi and spend whatever she needed but to get receipts because the situation might turn into an actual case.

Mary looked at the amount of money and shook her head and asked what she thought a taxi was going to cost.

Aurea asked if Alex was going to find her parents.

Alex sat down at the table and put her hands on Aurea's hands and said that she was going to do everything possible to find them but while she was looking Aurea would be staying in a room in the house and would be kept safe. She should plan on going to school, then to the library afterwards and that later they would all have dinner either at the house or at a restaurant.

She then said that she and Johnnie were leaving, and that Mary was going to make sure she got to school and afterwards to the library.

She looked at Mary and asked her to find out what she could from the teachers and the librarians.

She followed Johnnie down the front steps to where they had their bikes chained.

The two talked back and forth via their headsets on their ride down the hill to the police station.

Once there, Alex stopped to get her cup of coffee before heading over to her desk.

She knew she was in for a quiz when Trevor smiled and asked why she was late for work.

Trey handed her half of a bear claw, and she slowly took a bite before replying to Trevor.

Johnnie walked in with his coffee, looked into the donut box, and picked out a glazed cake donut.

She smiled and replied to Trevor's question that she had been looking for a suitable case that they could work on, and she was going to make sure he got the exciting end.

Trevor laughed and said that he had never figured out what end the dull part of any of her cases happened to be.

The Chief came over and suggested that she, Johnnie, and Trey accompany him into his office.

Bill laughed and said that it seemed that they were going to be left out.

The Chief looked over to him and said that he should be glad to be able to relax while he ate his donut and had his coffee.

Once in the office, the Chief asked Alex to explain the situation. He made the point that parents dropping kids off to a stranger for safe keeping was very unusual. He stated that he was going to treat it as a formal case that involved potential danger. He said that he had already informed his bosses and they all agreed that given the history of your cases it was warranted.

Alex shook her head and asked what they meant by the history of her cases.

He asked her how many times she had been shot and ended up in the hospital.

She nodded and said that it was more times than she cared to think about.

He handed her the folder that was labeled, "The package on the front porch case."

She read the label and laughed. She said that it was the most beautiful package that she had recently seen. It had dark brown eyes, auburn hair, and a honey-colored skin and it was well composed and polite. She knew she was from Brazil but had yet to follow up on that.

The Chief smiled and said that she should make sure that she did not get too attached to that beautiful package.

He asked her how she planned to proceed.

She said that the place she was going to start was the hole in the wall diner just a few blocks away. Then she was going to the Cincinnati Library and talk to some librarians and finally she was going to walk to where Aurea went to school and see if she could talk with Aurea's teachers. She said that by the late afternoon she hoped to figure out how she would proceed.

She added that she had Mary was looking after Aurea and probably talking to some of the same people.

The Chief then asked if she planned to leverage the rest of the team.

Alex smiled and said that she would love to as soon as she had something for them to do but at the moment, she was not sure what that might be.

He nodded and looked at Trey and simply said, "have her back."

Trey smiled and asked if he meant "hold her back."

The Chief laughed and said for him to do both.

Alex smiled, waved her case folder, and walked out of the office.

She walked over to where Bill and Trevor were sitting having their morning coffee and asked them if they wanted to come along and enjoy brunch at a small local restaurant.

Trevor nodded and said that he would love to but that she had to lead the way into the restaurant because he did not want to be asked along just to serve as a shield.

Bill gave Trevor a shove and said that the next time bullets flew he was going to stand behind him.

Alex led the team to the small restaurant. She and Johnnie had made it a point to try breakfast and lunch at almost all the downtown establishments. This particular one had been visited once but had never made it to their favorite list.

She walked in and was greeted by the same person who had served her before. She asked for a table for five.

He smiled and said that he was pleased that she had decided to come back. He asked her to be patient because his normal waitress was absent.

Alex put in her order for tea and a scone and once the orders were in, she asked where the waitress that was absent had gone.

The owner said that she and her husband had an early morning breakfast and as they were finishing a large rather rude man came in and spoke to them in a foreign language. Then the waitress got up gave him a hug and followed the man out to his car.

He said that he followed them out to door, and that he got a picture of the license plate. He pulled out his phone and pulled up the picture.

Johnnie took the phone and sent the picture to all of them. He looked over at Trevor and asked him to follow up on it.

Alex asked the proprietor what language the rude person had used.

He shook his head and said that it was not Spanish but seemed similar.

A few moments later, Trevor's phone buzzed. He kept saying, "yes, yes, OK," and then hung up.

He looked around and said that the car was a rental that had been rented at the airport.

Alex asked that he and Bill follow up and see if it was still out and if not see if they could find out to what airline the renter had gone to. She added that the car should be impounded so that forensics could go over it in detail and get fingerprints and DNA.

Trevor nodded and said that he was glad that so far, he and Bill got the easy end of the case.

Alex smiled and said that they should get going while the trail was hot and to make sure neither of them got shot.

Once they had left, she looked at Trey and Johnnie and said that she was beginning to think that they would not find Aurea's parents alive. She hoped that she was wrong but to have someone come to Cincinnati from Brazil to meet with them felt ominous to her.

She wondered what the two had been running from. She looked at Johnnie and asked if he could look them up on some database that would have their visa information. And if he could follow their names to wherever it might lead.

She was quiet for a moment then asked Trey whether she could bring Aurea to his grill out on Sunday.

Trey nodded and said that he had just gone through all the toys that Nolan had outgrown. He was planning to pass them on to friends or give away. He figured he had plenty that might interest Aurea but there would be no kids her age to play with at the grill out.

Alex smiled and said that Matt was coming along and would fill in.

She then suggested they go to the library and see what they could learn there.

Johnnie nodded, said that he still had many librarian friends that he was sure would have noticed Aurea and might have some information that might prove useful.

Several librarians knew Aurea and commented that she was a bright young girl that must have been related to Johnnie because she always made sure to attend the lectures that had refreshments provided.

That gave Johnnie a laugh. He added that no one as pretty as Aurea would be a relative of his.

He asked what other things that Aurea was into and learned that Aurea loved to do research on the internet and by research she was into researching famous individuals and the histories of various countries.

Trey asked if that was common for someone so young and learned that it was not and that was why it was being mentioned.

Alex asked about Aurea's parents and learned that Aurea's mother would sign her in and then leave for work. She would return on time to sign Aurea out and take her home. It was clear that the mother took very good care of her daughter and the two of them were close.

Alex thanked each of the librarians and then took a moment to summarize that they had learned that Aurea loved the treats she could get at the library, and she was into learning about the history of the world around her. She added that the treats would be attractive to any kid but Aurea arranged her time so she could enjoy one each day. She was also a serious young lady in that she was into studying history and famous people.

Back in the office, Johnnie focused on getting into the database that would have the visa information for Aurea's parents. He also ran the face recognition program against the news databases in Sao Paulo. It did not take long for him to find a couple of articles that had Bento's picture. Several times he was standing behind the ring leaders of a drug distribution ring that controlled most of Sao Paulo.

Once again Alex commented that she was feeling more and more like they would not find either Janaina or Bento alive. She wondered if either of the two ring leaders might be the one that had left the diner with the two.

She asked Johnnie to go back with a picture of the two and see if the diner's proprietor recognized either of them. She also asked him to send the pictures out to Bill and Trevor to see if any of the ticket agents recognized either of the two.

She led the way to the school that Aurea attended and once there she introduced herself and the fact that she was trying to find out what she could about Aurea's mother and father. She did not learn much but was asked to clarify the fact that Aurea was accompanied to school by a Mary Higgins, and she wanted confirmation that everything was legal and appropriate.

Alex assured her that Aurea was being looked after while she tried to locate her mother and father.

She was then able to talk to several of the teachers that had nothing but praise for Aurea, her behavior, and her high standing in all of her classes.

She unexpectedly felt sense of pride in the positive information she was learning about Aurea.

After returning to the office, she was sitting at her desk when Bill and Travis returned from the airport and said that they had struck pay dirt in that one of the ticket agents recalled one of the men in the pictures and called him a rude dude because he was upset that he couldn't get a first-class seat.

He was headed for the Grand Canyon and was traveling on a one-way ticket. The agent conjectured that he must be leaving from that airport on a ticket of some other airline but when he had asked about helping to make a good connection, he had been told to mind his own business.

Alex asked Trevor and Bill if they wanted to join in on an evening dinner at a restaurant of Johnnie's choice.

Both of them said that they had other plans for the evening.

Trey spoke up and said that he preferred to go home to dinner.

Matt was still out with his EMT team at dinner time, so Alex, Johnnie, Mary, and Aurea went to dinner at a restaurant that had a great view of the River Front Park's play area and the John A. Roebling Suspension Bridge that crossed the river to Covington.

Aurea was immediately drawn to the window and said that she saw a couple of places where she had played. She turned away from the window and then asked whether Alex had found her mother.

Alex said that she had not.

After ordering dinner, Alex shared the fact that everyone that she had talked to had said nice things about Aurea. She asked Aurea if she would like to go with her and Matt to a grill out at Trey's house.

Aurea asked if there would be any other kids there.

Alex shook her head and said that there would be no kids but plenty of toys, an outdoor swing set and plenty of great food.

Aurea nodded and said, "OK."

187

Thank You for reading this far. Go to remwriter95.net to purchase the book.

https://www.remwriter95.net/

<u>About the Author</u>

Ron Mueller
<u>remwriter95.net/</u>

Ron grew up in what is now Flint River State Park in Southeast Iowa. The 170-year-old house Ron lived in is built into a hillside. It faces a 125-foot-high cliff towering over the little Flint River. The house and the land talked to him about; the passing of time, the struggle to conquer the land, the struggles people faced and the wonder of nature.

He climbed the cliffs, crawled into the caves, dove from the swimming rock, collected clams from the bottom of the pond, gigged and skinned frogs for their legs. He trapped muskrats for fur, hunted raccoon in the dead of night, and with only a stick hunted rabbits in the dead of winter.

His young life was outdoors, and nature tested him.

He walked to a one room stone schoolhouse uphill both ways. A stern but warm-hearted teacher, Mrs. Henry was instrumental in shaping his character as she shepherded him from the fourth to the eighth grade.

It was a great way to grow up.

Ron graduated from Burlington, High School, went to Vietnam in the Navy. He graduated from The University of South Florida with a master's degree in engineering, worked for thirty eight years for Procter and Gamble, traveled around the world thirty times.

He has remained happily married for more than fifty years. His daughter and his two sons are all successful and his three grandchildren have all graduated.

His wife has humored and supported him as he became a full time professional story teller.

He has come to realize that he is, what is known as, a Cozy writer. Excitement and adventure but little guts and gore. His heroine or hero suffer a little but live happily ever after.

His experiences inter-twined with snippets of fantasy lend themselves to the adventures he leads the reader through.

Books by Ron Mueller

Fiction Series
The Alex Evercrest Series
The River Front
The Girl on The Grill
Missing
Maggot
Racist
Votive Candles
Windy City
Country Road
Pool of Blood
Sins of the Daughter
Body Parts
The Skull Collector
The Vanishing
The Shadow Fighter
Moonshine
Grief's Trajectory
The Magic Touch
Northern Lights
Alex Evercrest Heroine
Alex Evercrest Collection Two
New Direction
A Family Affair
Disruption
The St. Lebuinnus Church Murder
A Brian O'Neil Novel
Hawaiian Phoenix
Moon Curser
Death Broker
The Problem Solver Series
Solutions
Drug Lords
Border Crosser
The Problem Solver Collection
The Taelo Series
The Early Years
The Golden Feather
Journey of Discovery
Dangerous Passage
Condor Clan Slingers
Circumvention
The Journey of Sages
Collection
Future Leaders Journey
A Taelo Story
White Swan and Quiet Pheasant
The Child's Name
Floating Cloud
Quiet Rabbit
Busy Bee
Little Otter & Talking Wren
Broken Spear
Burley Bear & Meadow Flower
Taelo Story Collection

<u>**Science Fiction**</u>

The Savitar Series:
Journey's End
Savitar
Confluence
Savitar Series Collection

The Door Series
The Door
Aliens We
The Endless Hole
The Swarm
Esoteric Journey
The Gentle Eye
The Door Series Collection

Bram Nielson Series
The Fold
The Message
Fold Wormhole
Negative Fold
Ripples in Time
Bram Nielson Collection

<u>**Single Science Fiction Books:**</u>
Current Past and Future
The Event
The Door
Viajante 7

https://www.remwriter95.net/

Characters in the Story

Alex	Cathy	Evercrest	Police Detective
Matthew	Timothy	Knolton	Alex's suitor
Rose-Anne	Germain	Evercrest	Alex's mother
Russel	Johnson	Evercrest	Alex's father
Helping Hands charity			Alex's nonprofit org
Trey		McGregor	Alex's Detective Partner
Lindsey		McGregor	Wife
Nolan		McGregor	Son
Johnnie		Smith	Old Viet Vet
Mary		Higgins	Johnnie's Phili "friend"
Bruce	Lincoln	Johnson	Cinci Chief of Detectives
Mary-Anne	Leslie	Johnson	Chiefs Wife
Bill	Hamilton	Danson	Detective
Travis	Bailey	Carter	Detective
Dr. Rogers			Coroner
Jane	Elousie	Stradford	Lieutenant Governor
Felix			proprietor at fishing dock
Golden Goose			Name of the Yacht
Sandra		Olson	Policewoman guard
Annie	Lorie	Scots	Missing girl
Linda		Annies	older daughter
Lorie		Annies	second daughter
Harold		Zimmerman	Chicago DEA
James	Oscor	Kaizer	Sheriff of Wiggin
Abbie	Alisa	Bender	protect Alex married James
John	S.	Williams	Lawyer that was abused
Hanna		Waverly	John's mate
Angelica			Angel on the hill
Brian		Lexter	Cinci FBI Bureau Chief
Cais		Leu	Alex's Viet friend
Tracy		Hunter	Trey's Analyst
Liam			CIA operative
Orson		Ambrose	Seattle captive
Sebastian		Cassidy	Seattle captive

Elisa	Amos	LA Captive
Mateo	Garcia	LA Captive
Thiago	Bandello	Sandiego Captive
Osvaldo	Comonte	Sandiego Captive
Riggs	Melville	Boston Captive
Rowan		Boston Captive
Ezekiel		New York Captive
Boaz		New York Captive
Dante	Cruz	Miami Captive
Kenji	Mochizuki	Miami Captive
Braylon	Corbyn	Chicago Captive
Mykel	Holmes	Chicago Captive
Zyair	Smith	St. Louis Captive
Lev	Gataki	St. Louis Captive
Ambrose		New Orleans Captive
Enzo	Beaufoy	New Orleans Captive
Jack	Ahearn	LA Leader Captive
Mylo		Miami Leader Captive
Harper	Bardin	New Orleans Ldr Captive
Laticia		CIA Agent
Thermon		CIA Agent
Jason		CIA Agent

https://www.remwriter95.net/

Published by: Around the World Publishing LLC.